A Better Place

A NOVEL

Bruce Blizard

AUTHOR OF GOD'S INSTANT

Design and Interior formatting services provided by:

A Better Place ...

Mothers know the part they play in the lives of their children. They give birth to us twice. The first is on the day we are born. Their bodies will not give us up until we're fully formed and able to survive as something more than greedy parasites that devour their strength and grow for nine months to an inconvenient size.

Some mothers, though they're rare, lament the loss of dependency and weep uncontrollably for days or even weeks. But most take a breath and marvel at the newly independent spirit they have struggled to squeeze into the crowded world. Those mothers also weep tears of joy at the unheard voice whispering of the glory that is the child and of the glory that may come as a result of the child. My mother felt the potential glory of my life urgently, and she would not allow anything or anyone to cloud or to alter it.

My mother lived to create in me a love for the things she loved. Books and poetry, our garden, and my father. She did not die until I was fully formed and ready to be released gloriously into the world for the second time. No one else mattered because no one else (not even my father) understood. All things happen for a reason. We are all going to a better place.

But something is set against us.

Dedication

I only lived in Pomeroy, Washington for two years, when I taught English at town's high school. But the people in that small eastern Washington community are among the best I've ever known. Kind and caring. Hardworking. The salt of the earth. And this book is dedicated to them

Acknowledgments

I need to thank Jim Deatherage, who read the manuscript in the early stages and made a generous and helpful critique of the "finished" product. I owe a tremendous debt to two outstanding professionals: Author and editor Jennifer Lynn (Ciotta) at Pencey X Pages (http://penceyxpages.com/) for her skillful and insightful editing; and Brett Grimes Brett Grimes Design who designs the covers for all my books. And of course, this project would not have been possible at all without my wife Tina who seems to understand why the work matters.

Chapter 1

Washington State Highway 128 climbs gently to the south away from the tiny town of Pomeroy. After seventeen miles the road becomes an anomaly on the map, the only state highway in Washington that is not paved. Twenty-five miles from town, even the gravel road ends at the boundary of the Umatilla National Forest. It's replaced by an unmapped network of dirt tracks, in some places barely wide enough for a single vehicle. Still, someone who knows the roads and understands the risks inherent to traveling in the mountains without a map can make his way through the Blue Mountains to the small towns in northeastern Oregon, like Elgin and Joseph, and from there link up with more civilized paved roads. Or a traveler familiar with the unmapped regions of the Blues, someone who desires anonymity, privacy, or escape could get so lost no one in authority would be willing to search very hard.

One very dark night in early autumn, a tall, angular sheriff named Tom Bennett parked his Garfield County SUV behind a horse trailer hitched to a familiar black-and-silver pickup parked in a narrow turnout deep in the Blue Mountain about a mile from the Oregon border. The right-side tires of the truck were far enough off the dirt siding, so the cab leaned awkwardly into the shallow ditch next to the road. The lights of Tom's police car shone past the trailer, and he could see no one was behind the wheel. After carefully double-checking the cab to make sure the truck was unoccupied, Tom walked to the rear of the trailer, parked carefully on level ground in the turnout. This was a habit of experienced horsemen who needed a flat spot to unload their horses. Tom nodded his approval then shone his flashlight over the closed tailgate. He could see it had been recently occupied by two horses.

As he stood in the headlights of his vehicle, he didn't notice that in the trees about two hundred feet uphill from the dirt roadway a man had the front site of a .30-.30 Winchester trained on Tom's right temple. A hundred feet farther back into the woods, a twelve-year-old girl mounted on one of the horses from the trailer held lightly to the reins of the other. She could not see the dirt road, the truck and trailer, or Tom. But she could see what her father was doing with his rifle. She was cold but not scared. She did not shiver or tremble because that might cause one of the horses to react with a snort, the stomp of a foot, or a light whinny. She understood the horses must remain silent because that was the last thing her father had said before he took his rifle from its scabbard and headed back down the hill toward the road.

Tom knew who the truck belonged to, and he knew why it was abandoned. He turned to shine his flashlight into the woods. It wouldn't penetrate more than fifty feet, so he stepped across the barrow pit and gingerly into the woods on the other side. He shone his light on the ground looking for hoof prints or any other sign that would reveal the general direction the horses had gone. As he did so, the man with the rifle lowered himself to one knee and thumbed off the safety. Tom's flashlight revealed nothing unusual, so he moved carefully another thirty feet from the road, first scanning the shadows up the hill and then the ground. He saw the deep impressions left by two horses working hard to get up the hill.

"Anyone there?" he asked as loud as he could without shouting. "Jake, this is not a great place to leave your rig. Ridin' into Oregon's not going to do you no good. When the authorities down there find you, they'll just send you back. If you can hear me, you best come on out and we'll talk about what you need to do."

Tom took several more tentative steps up the hill, listening hard. He stopped and peered into the trees as he slowly shifted the flashlight from his right hand to his left and back again. There was no moon, and thick clouds promised rain and hid the stars. The man with the rifle moved the crosshairs of his scope to a spot on Tom's chest about twelve inches above the flashlight.

"Don't come any closer," he whispered. "One more step and I got to shoot you, Tom. Please go back."

Tom could feel the weight of the mountains, which rose steeply away from both sides of the narrow roadway, beginning to close in on him. He thought for a long moment and decided it would be foolish to pursue anyone into the woods on foot at night and alone, especially when they were likely to be mounted and even more likely to have ridden down into Oregon by now. Tom knew the mountains well enough to know that stumbling around in the dark chasing an armed man made no sense.

"OK, Jake," he said, wondering if anyone in the dark forest was close enough to hear. "I'm going to call the state patrol and tell 'em I found your rig."

Tom turned quickly and went back to his SUV to make the call. By midday the truck and trailer would be gone. So would the man with the rifle and his daughter and both horses.

The girl's name was June. Her father was Jake. The fact his rig would be gone and the fact the state patrol would soon know where he'd been did not concern him. He intended to remain out of sight for a good long time. As long, in fact, as it took to get himself and the girl far enough away that no one would know who they were or why they were traveling through the mountains on horseback at night.

Jake watched until Tom got into his car. While the sheriff made his call on the radio, Jake silently made his way back to where June waited with the two horses. He approached the girl carefully and patted her on the leg.

"You did real good, Honey. Now we got to get a couple of hours farther on before we can rest. Stay close behind me and trust your horse and we'll be just fine."

June understood. Her life to that point had taught her to trust her father in all difficult circumstances.

"I'll be fine, Dad," she said in a whisper. It had always been "Dad," never "Daddy." Then she said, "We ought to get movin'. I don't think we want to travel in the daylight, not for a while at least."

"Good girl," Jake said.

He walked around the back of June's horse, checking the cinches and rigging out of habit. He squeezed between the two horses and walked to the front of his own mount. He stroked the stout bay gelding on the neck, twisted the left stirrup around, stepped up, and spun himself into the saddle. Without a word, he turned his horse away from his daughter and headed quietly up the hill deeper into the woods.

A light rain began to fall as June followed her father.

Chapter 2

My name is June, and I was the girl on the horse.

Now I'm someone different. Just like everyone else.

This is the story of my mother and my father. And maybe of a man I met in the mountains. The story doesn't really start out badly for me. But it looks that way, riding away from that dirt road into the dark and toward a strange country, with the rain coming, but it ends up in a better place.

We all end in a better place.

I got here thanks to my father, and before that, thanks to my mother, who died a few weeks before we rode into the wilderness of the Blue Mountains. So, this is really my parents' story.

Some people said it was a terrible thing for my father to take a twelve-year-old girl away from home and into the mountains at night, to hide her from the rest of the world. The same people said our home was not a fit place for me. But my father, who is still the best man I've ever known, was keeping a promise to my mother, whose only rules were that he should keep me safe and tell the truth. My father once had a problem with the truth, not with telling the truth, but with recognizing it. But my mother…well, my mother came from the "the rest of the world" where the truth can get you in trouble. She wanted more than anything for me to live in the truth, and so beyond the rest of the world.

Now they have to let me go, and I'm going to try.

My story begins near the little town of Pomeroy, Washington. Pomeroy is one of those little working towns in eastern Washington state that more sophisticated people in places like Seattle and Bellingham misunderstand (deliberately, my mother would say). People in Pomeroy are proud to say the town is thirty miles in every direction from any other place that matters. Thirty miles from Dayton, another small town to the west. Thirty miles from Clarkston in Washington and Lewiston in Idaho to the east. Thirty miles from the Snake River to the north. And thirty miles from the Oregon border where it dissects the wilderness of the Blue Mountains and the Wallowa Country to the south. Fewer than a thousand people lived in Pomeroy in those days. And the town still seems settled into a more reasonable past time, which is why my parents chose to live south of the town on the extreme verge of the rolling wheat country of the Palouse Hills and the ancient and sacred wilderness of the Wallowa Range.

My mother inherited the house we lived in only because her own parents, particularly her mother, had no use for mountains or wilderness or livestock. It was built in the 1880s by one of the first settlers in the area. It was passed down in her family from generation to generation until no one was left who wanted to live there. The last progeny of the original owner was a great-aunt, whom my mother barely knew. Still, as the old woman neared the end of her life, she took great care to leave the house and 720 acres of rugged pastureland and forest to someone who would live there and keep the land, as closely as possible, "in the family." When she was satisfied that my mother and her young family (I was five years old when we moved onto the old place) would be able to preserve the house and care for the land, and as soon as she saw my parents safely settled into the old house, my mother's old aunt moved to Walla Walla. She died there in less than a month.

Whenever my mother told me the story of how she'd met and married my father and how we acquired the house and the land, the general drift of the tale was always the same. But each time there was a deliberate and discernible difference: she'd shift the point of view, leave out a snippet of conversation, or add a word or two of her own commentary. It was as if the story seemed to float with the current of what was on her mind at the time, with what she knew I needed from the story at any particular moment. My mother seemed to enjoy the idea of being part of something very old. My father had been shocked and saddened by the old woman's death (I think he felt responsible), but my mother had expected her great-aunt to die and understood. She tried to make sure I understood.

"Why would she want to live anywhere else," my mother would ask when some word passed through a conversation to remind me of the old woman. "She knows we're on the land. That was enough for her. It was time. She's in a better place now."

Everyone says "she's or he's in a better place" when someone dies. It makes people feel less desperate I suppose. It softens the blow and suggests an inkling of hope for when their own time comes. But my mother meant it. She also meant it when she said the same thing about her own approaching death years later.

"I'm going to a better place. We all are. And soon."

My mother always told the truth, and I think she hoped my father would finally believe. I'm not completely sure he ever did, but he kept faith with what she believed about this world and the next and with what she wanted for me. He could have taken an easier road, the road everyone else takes. He may have even thought the easy road was the best one for me, but he trusted my mother.

My father was the kind of man who saw things in the hard, clear, practical light of the working day. What mattered most was what needed to be done soonest, and all things were assigned a value based on their immediate usefulness. For my mother, though, practical matters would take care of themselves, mostly because she had my father to take care of them. Insight mattered to her. Intuition mattered. An invisible, intangible reality mattered. Why a thing was to be done mattered as much as how a thing was to be done.

We always had horses. In those days it was just easier to get around the Blue Mountains on horseback. There were few roads, and we didn't go to town very often. My father's way with horses was not patient. He expected a young horse to understand what was required of him, and if the animal did not understand quickly, he would use spurs or a rope or a short tie-down to help him understand. His aim was to break a young horse, to make him useful. When my father was done with a horse, my mother would "gentle" him. Talk to him. Stroke him. Caress him. Her aim was to treat a young horse filled with desire, spirit, and heart something like a promising child, or like her doubting husband.

"You can't treat a horse or anyone else that way for very long," she'd tell my father. "You've got to make him trust you. He'll do what you want if he trusts you."

My father's reply was always the same: "I reckon he can trust that he's gonna do what I say."

My mother and father would never argue beyond this point. They knew the truth rested uneasily somewhere on both ends of the issue, and that, while the truth is the same for all time, it is not the same for all horses. They had settled into an unspoken agreement about the best way to make a horse useful.

In the same way, my father taught me the practical things a child needed to know to live on our place. I learned early that essential tasks cannot be put off or delayed. There was no supermarket, no mechanic down the road to rescue us. I could ride nearly as well as my father by the time I was seven or eight. By the time I was ten, I could chop wood, sight a rifle, and move our small herd of cattle up from the pine-shaded valley pastures at the south end of our land into the corral near the house. There we'd feed them up so they'd be ready for market or for our own freezer. Long before we left for the wilderness of the Blue Mountains and long before my mother died, I'd learned when to rest a horse and how to keep our ancient pickup running. I knew the difference between a hackamore and a snaffle, and I understood oil changes and sparkplugs. My father was suspicious of neediness, so he taught me how to survive on my own.

My mother read to me even before I could sit up in her lap. She told me old stories from her substantial family history, stories left behind in journals and letters stored in three handmade wooden boxes and left behind on the kitchen table for my mother to find on the day we moved in. Little was ever said about her own parents except that her mother didn't care for the old stories. We read the Bible and Shakespeare and Thoreau together, and she recited Edgar Allen Poe and Emily Dickinson to me. She had carefully researched the history of our home place and seemed to be able to identify every rock, tree, and leaf—not necessarily by name but by function or location. She taught me first to mend my clothes and then how to sew well enough to make my own new clothes. She cooked and baked and kept the house in repair. And I learned, first by watching her and later by doing the work myself.

I am a hybrid, a product of the best parts of each of my parents. And the worst.

We all are.

Past and present, reason and desire, hard-scrabble reality and whimsy live together in my memory of those days. So, when my father aimed his gun at the sheriff, I knew and understood why, as a practical matter, he would pull the trigger. But I also prayed and believed God would not make it necessary.

Chapter 3

June began her day before the late-rising sun finally climbed over the nearby hills. She was often awake before her parents and was usually shivering with a book at the kitchen table by 6:00 a.m. At that time her parents came down the narrow stairway that opened into the kitchen, which, typically, was by far the largest room in the old house. Her father would rekindle the fire in the corner stove while her mother moved to a very old electric range to begin breakfast. Then her father would shrug into a heavy coat and go outside to take care of the nearby animals, a young milk cow and two saddle horses. While her father was outside, June would close her book and help her mother put breakfast on the table. When he returned, breakfast would be ready, and the family would eat together.

"June, I need you to go down to the south-end pastures with me." When her father spoke, June read to the end of a paragraph and then closed her book while he waited. She would remember her place when he was done. "There's some extra cows down there and I need to get them close to the house until we find out who they belong to."

She folded her hands on the hard cover of the book and thought for a moment when Jake was done speaking.

"Are they Herefords?" she asked. "Because there was a big herd of Herefords down along the border. Maybe a couple of those cows wandered up here after the rest were rounded up and shipped."

"Maybe. But I don't want anyone thinking we're keeping those cows. We'll find out who they belong to, but I still need you to help me bring 'em up. Your mom says she has work to do in the house."

"I don't think Herefords would do very good…"

"Very *well*," Sarah, her mother, said.

June sighed quietly and began again. "I don't think Herefords would do very *well* in that country because they'd have to move around too much to find feed."

"There's a lot of Herefords up in the north end of the county," Jake said. "A little grass grows in the wheat stubble and the Herefords do just fine on it. I 'spect someone down in Oregon got an idea to graze some of those red cows in the little valleys down that way, just to see how they'd do. My guess is they loaded 'em up and hauled 'em down to the feedlots in Lagrande or maybe Baker City, and a few got lost and left behind."

"It seems like grazing cattle in those hills wouldn't fatten them up much."

"We'll see how they look when we see 'em up close. There's only about a half dozen. We'll drive 'em up near to the house, and I'll ask around town to see if anyone from Oregon is missing any red cows."

Sarah had the table cleared by the time they had finished talking. Jake left to saddle the horses so he and June could get started.

"June," she said. "What were you reading this morning?"

"A myth, 'Cupid and Psyche.' About the princess and the beautiful god she's not allowed to see even though she's married to him."

"Where else have you seen a story like that?"

"I don't know for sure, but it seems familiar."

"And where do most familiar stories come from?"

The girl did not answer right away. She knew the answer, or at least she knew what her mother wanted to hear.

"The Bible. The stories all come from the Bible. But isn't this story older than the Bible? Didn't the people who told this story in Greece come before the Bible?"

Sarah smiled at the girl. She was proud that her daughter knew something about where books came from.

"How does your father know how to take care of his cows? Or, how does Mr. Luke up north know when to plant his wheat and when to harvest?"

"I guess they must've read it in a book."

"Maybe. But I've never seen your father read a book. The truth is that people have known how to take care of their animals and how to grow their crops for a lot longer than there have been books."

June opened her book to the page where she'd stopped and stared at the words without reading. She put her left hand on the right-hand page and touched it gently with her fingertips, as if it were a newly hatched chick or newborn calf, delicate and fragile. Then she closed her eyes and thought hard for a long moment.

"The people in the Bible knew the stories before they were written down," she said. "And the Greek people knew about 'Cupid and Psyche' before that story was put into a book."

"That's right, June. The stories come first and from long ago. Books come later."

"Then which stories are true?"

Sarah got up from the table and went to the sink to begin washing the breakfast dishes. She loved the feeling of the hot water when she reached into the sink and started to work. She rubbed the soap against the back of her hands, another essential luxury, as she thought about June's question. She did not answer.

"Mom, are some of the stories true and some not?"

"They are all true in a way. Each story tells a piece of the truth. Maybe the princess in your story can't see what her love looks like because she can never really know what's in his heart. We only know people on the outside, really. Maybe she's meant to know his heart before she knows what he looks like."

"Jesus said something like that, didn't he?"

"Yes, I think he did. See, all the stories come back to the Bible if you follow them long enough."

Jake plodded into the house.

"Get ready to go, June. These cows aren't the only thing I've got to attend to today."

The ranch Sarah inherited was five sections, five square miles in a nearly perfect rectangle and more than a mile and a half across. It was where the vast wheat fields of the Palouse Hills gave way to the nearly pristine wilderness of the Blue Mountains in Washington and the Wallowa Country in the remote northeastern corner of Oregon. The house was nestled onto the only level location on the property, several miles south of Garfield County's last wheat field.

The "highway" from Pomeroy into the mountains changed from pavement to gravel after meandering for fifteen miles south of town. At a bend in the gravel road more than twenty-five miles from town, a narrow dirt track wound to the left through the sparse pines. After climbing for almost a mile, the dirt track crested a low ridge and slid through a sturdy gate with a tight five-strand barbed-wire fence running off in both directions. From there, after another half mile on the same track, the house sat beside an ancient orchard planted by the original occupant. There was no fence around the yard and only hard-packed dirt where a lawn might have been. Jake had rebuilt the sagging front porch and painted the house a useful gray, and Sarah had installed flower boxes in the yard and under each of the four small front windows.

For June's mother, the isolation and solitude were a welcome change from the life she'd known. For June's father, life on the ranch was the perfect complement to his solitary disposition. And the girl had never known anything else.

The home was powered by a single electrical line that stretched overland on very old poles from the end of the paved section of the highway to the northeast corner of the house. It was a necessary concession to the outside world. But there was no television and no radio, and the family did not read newspapers or magazines. They knew people in town, but the precise location of the ranch, or the fact the ranch was even occupied, was unknown to all but a necessary handful of people. Its existence was not even imagined by anyone from outside.

*

Sarah came to the ranch from the opposite corner of Washington. She was born in Bellingham, an old town factionalized and alienated between its lumber mill past and college town present. Her own parents, both professors at Western Washington State College when she was born, were determined to have only one child and to make as much of that child as possible.

At school, Sarah was always the best student in her class. She was reading Mark Twain in kindergarten and doing calculus by the fifth grade. In her young mind, life was as it should be. She had been raised to be her parents' legacy, the natural consequence of her English professor father's frequent appearance in scholarly journals and her mother's unique place as one of the school's first female mathematics professors. The girl understood she was the progeny of unique people and accepted her own exceptionality as a matter of inevitable fact.

"Sarah," her kindergarten teacher said on the first day of school. "Would you like to show us how well you know your letters?"

"No, I would not," the precocious four-year-old said. "Everyone knows their letters. I can't remember when I didn't know my letters."

From that day forward, it was obvious that Sarah would never be a part of the life of her peers. The girl accepted that fact as the natural consequence of her uniqueness, but others outside the family were worried that she would pass through her childhood with no friends at all.

"Mother," she begged at the end of that first day. "I don't want to go back to school. The other children don't know anything."

"Child of mine," her mother answered. "The other children don't matter. I wish there was another way. But you must go to school. And you must try to treat the teachers kindly. They will very soon recognize what you are, and special arrangements will be made."

But no special arrangements were made, so every evening Sarah would sit at a desk in her room and work two or three or four years ahead of wherever her class happened to be. The math was easy, so the girl begged to spend more time with books and poetry. To her father's delight, she loved the poets of the nineteenth century, especially Poe when she was very young and Emily Dickinson later.

Her mother would have preferred she spend this time on number theory or calculus. But she recognized and was proud of the rare literary talent possessed by her daughter, so she did not discourage her love of books. Sarah remained in school but was bored. She learned to do what was expected through the early grades and middle school, and she learned it was best not to seem to know more than the teacher. She sat apart when she could. She did not make friends.

She was special.

By the time she was about to enter high school, even her parents had become concerned that she did not socialize well. Not that she was defiant or rebellious or that she was disliked by other children, but she seemed not to need the companionship of others at all, children or adults. This, of course, was a constant source of concern for her teachers and others who observed her at school, so annual meetings were held with Sarah's parents.

The very first meeting, on a cold January day when Sarah was in the second grade, was typical of all those to follow. Every day Sarah would get done with her work very early. Then she would sit at her desk and tap her pencil and hum or sing loudly enough for the other kids to be either distracted or to join in. Her behavior caused the teacher to scold her and insist she sit quietly until the other children were done. After several similar episodes, the girl's parents were called in.

"Sarah is a very bright girl," the teacher said. "But she doesn't seem to understand she must sit quietly while the other children are working."

"Can we send reading material or extra work for her to do when she is done with your work?" her mother asked.

"I don't think that would be appropriate," the teacher said. "Other parents would want special work for their students. It's important the class move forward together."

"Then," her father said. "Is there work in the room she could do until everyone else is finished."

"No!" The teacher paused and took a shallow breath. She was becoming impatient. "It really is necessary for Sarah to sit quietly when her work is done. As I said, Sarah is very bright, quite advanced really, but if she's going to succeed in school, she needs to learn to play along and not be disruptive."

Sarah's parents said they understood and would speak to the girl. Sarah agreed to try. "But really, Mother, the other kids are so slow."

A similar meeting took place at least once every year until she was in high school. She entered high school as a thirteen-year-old with no friends and no desire to have any. But her life at Bellingham High was to be nothing like her earlier school life.

Perhaps that was why June would say many years later that her mother insisted on only two indispensable facts: We are all going to a better place. And all things happen for a reason, and always for a good reason.

*

When June was very young, Sarah decided her daughter would have a very limited experience of the world she had known growing up, and to her mother's credit, June could not conceive of a better place than the family's remote ranch.

Their life on the ranch was a sanctuary for Sarah, a wooded cloister where she could live an austere, contemplative life free from the burden of her intellect. Jake could be completely self sufficient. Both her parents brought ulterior motives to the mountains, and the ranch was a place to be at rest. But for June the ranch was the locus of all she knew, all she understood, and all she was coming to believe.

Home.

She inhabited the place more completely than either of her parents. Her mother had tried to explain that most people did not live the way they did, but June simply could not believe that everyone did not live as well her family did.

When the breakfast dishes had been cleared and while her father was outside saddling the horses, June returned to her book. Following

Sarah's advice and example, she did not read quickly. She scanned each line slowly, her eyes stopping for a moment on words she was unsure of or curious about. Her mind recorded the text at what she thought was the rate it had been written, and she habitually paused to re-read difficult, interesting, or significant passages.

Every morning, she was completely dressed before she left her small upstairs room, so she was ready to go when Jake returned from saddling the horses.

"June, honey," he said as he came back into the room. "Get your hat, we gotta go."

She followed him outside to a sturdy corral behind the house. Jake's tall sorrel gelding and the slightly smaller bay mare June usually rode were tied to a heavy fence rail near the house. Both horses were veterans. "They've been there and done that," her father would say. They were unlikely to be spooked by anything they encountered on the one-hour ride to the southern end of the ranch. Sarah was a knowledgeable horsewoman, but June had rarely seen her on horseback. But the girl knew her mother wanted her to learn as much horse lore and horsemanship as possible. She possessed her father's firm way with a horse, but like her mother, she also knew intuitively why a horse would sometimes misbehave or refuse a task. Even as a young girl, June was no passive passenger. This was also as Sarah intended. Even though there wasn't much June could not do on a horse, Jake still waited until she was safely aboard to mount. He always made a quick walk around her horse to double-check the straps, buckles, and cinches. He would then stroke the mare's nose and whisper something reassuring in her ear before he mounted his own horse.

"Dad, it's OK. You just saddled the horses. There's no need to recheck everything. I'm not going to fall off."

"It never hurts to be careful. Only takes a minute."

Once he was satisfied that everything was secure, they rode at a slow walk through the open back gate of the corral. The wide cattle trail they followed rose away from the house and the corral then made a long-left turn along the low shoulder of a ridge before it dropped away more steeply into a narrow canyon. This would form a natural chute to guide the cows back over the ridge and into the corral when they returned.

As soon as Jake and June were out of sight, a tall wearing sturdy denim pants and a new red-and-green flannel shirt with the sleeves rolled up, emerged from the trees and walked swiftly to the house. He shifted the leather pouch over his left shoulder, stepped up onto the back porch, and knocked on the door.

The Blue Mountains had changed little since the days when Sarah's distant uncle first settled the land in the dying years of the nineteenth century. The cattle trail was one of nature's few concessions to the presence of people or livestock. On either side of the trail the forest sloped gently upward for a quarter of a mile before the mountains took over and the terrain steepened sharply, and the already sparse underbrush disappeared. The south end of the property consisted of a series of meadows lying at the bottom of three narrow valleys.

The meadows were insufficient to support cattle on a commercial scale, but Jake and his family kept eight mixed-breed cows and one rangy bull to provide plentiful meat and meager income. The bull stayed in a one-acre pasture near the house. When his services were needed, Jake and June would bring the cows up to the corral. When Jake was satisfied the bull had done his duty, he'd put the bull back in his own pasture and leave the back gate to the corral open so the cows would find their way back to the south end of the ranch. They'd graze until the first snow made it necessary to bring them back up to the barn and the corral for the winter.

Jake often wondered if it would be a good idea to enlarge his tiny herd. The money the extra calves would bring each year would come in handy. He might be able to buy feed for the winter instead of exchanging labor for cash and hay with Ed Luke. Ed Luke operated a large wheat and cattle operation at the far northern end of the county, hard by the Snake River and nearly as remote as their place, but much better known. Ed ran the largest commercial ranch in the county. Every fall he needed hands to harvest his wheat and drive trucks to the ancient steel-sided grain elevator that had marked the eastern city limits of Pomeroy for as long as anyone could remember. The biggest challenge he faced every year was keeping his machinery running. A breakdown would cost him time, and in the wheat business, timing was everything. That was where Jake came in. There didn't seem to be a problem with a piece of farm machinery or auto mechanics that he could not identify and fix. So valuable was Jake to Ed's operation that Ed paid him the same wage as the rest of his autumn crew and added fifty tons of good alfalfa hay just to keep Jake coming back every year.

The money from Ed Luke allowed Jake to pay his family's minimal utility bills and provide the few commodity items that the family could not produce at home. And the hay ensured his livestock would be well fed through the winter.

June and Jake rode quietly through the canyon, which opened into the first of the three shallow valleys. Neither their own cows nor the red strays were in the first valley.

"I guess that would've been too easy," he said. "Let's go around the ridge over here to the west. It's an easier ride, and that's the direction they would've come from."

"But there's no water in there," she said. "I believe we'll find them along that little stream to the east. It's likely to be the only water down here this time of year, and they'll be more green forage."

"I reckon you're right, girl. I was thinkin' of saving the horses. We'll go straight up to the top of the east ridge real slow and easy. We should be able to see them if they're in there. It's a small space, and a bunch a red cows'll be hard to miss. If they ain't watering on that little stream, we can ride on down to the south end of the ridge and across to the western coulee."

"Yes, sir," she said with a giggle. "Good plan, Dad."

It took about twenty minutes of slow climbing for the horses to reach the crest of the ridge. At the top, they dismounted and scanned the floor of the narrow valley for red cows.

"I don't see nothin'," he said. "I can see good clear across to the top of the next ridge, but I don't see no cows."

"There!" She pointed to a grove of very scraggly pine trees directly below them. "They're bunched up in those trees."

"Good eyes. Young eyes anyway. They'll be nice and rested for the trip back to the home place. I don't see our cows anywhere, though."

"They like to rest up in the shade at the north end of the canyon."

"Well, we always find them when we need to. I guess if they're off somewhere else, we won't have to worry about keeping them separate from this bunch. Let's go down and get 'em."

"Yes, sir!"

They remounted and rode into the canyon to a spot just north of the small Hereford herd.

"I see six," he said. "I thought there might be one or two more."

"If they're farm cows, they'd make easy prey for coyotes or a bear."

"You go on down the hill a bit and keep them from turning up the valley toward our cows. I doubt these critters have been drove much, so we got to take it slow. When we get to the end down there to the south, make sure you stay wide enough to turn them back up toward the canyon. Once we get them moving north, they'll pretty much find their own way home."

"I know. I'll be where you need me."

By early afternoon, they were following the six red cows over the last low ridge and into the corral by the house.

Sarah had seen them coming and was waiting to close the gate.

"Any problems?" she asked as she swung the gate closed and secured it with a short length of chain.

"Nope," he said. "Everyone did their job. June, give me your horse and I'll get 'em put away."

"Mom, is my book still on the table?"

Chapter 4

It's almost as if something were set against us.

Not the town. Not the people in the town, though at the time, I thought they might be in some way responsible. I was wrong.

"Sometimes evil seems so right, that the best you can do is back away from it," my mother told me shortly before her death. "It looks so good or sounds so appealing, no one questions it. When you come across a notion that no one questions, you have to step away, get a good look, but never take your eyes off it. Then find some place where it will forget you."

Everyone's parents live long, sometimes compelling lives before we come along. I don't think most children realize that.

My memories of my mother are clear and solid, like the secure fence of the corral built by my father, with posts that seemed to reach into the very heart of the Earth or the high walls of the narrow canyons where we could hide from the outside world. But my memories are incomplete because she left us just as my childhood was ending. I would have loved the opportunity to ask her about her own childhood. This stories were too recent to hold much truth for my mother. It will fall to another to tell the story of my mother's childhood.

I think my mother may have arranged the early years of my life to serve as a counterweight to her own childhood, as if she were determined to restore balance to the cosmic order.

What I knew then of my mother's short life begins when she met my father. It's as if I see my mother through a narrow window. The pane is clear, the image undistorted, but the view is incomplete. Her life before I was born is as much a mystery to me as all that was to come to her after she died, as if there are two eternities. My father would say we came to our home in the Blue Mountains because of my mother's good fortune, and that he was grateful to be married to a lucky woman. When he would talk that way, my mother would just bow her head and say "It's not luck. We're here because of God's deliberate and intentional good grace."

After all that's happened, I'm not sure *I* know what grace means. But I'm sure what *she* meant by grace. My mother didn't mind leaving this world. She didn't count her own death as loss. The loss was my father's and mine, not hers.

Mothers know the part they play in the lives of their children. They give birth to us twice. The first is on the day we are born. Their bodies will not give us up until we're fully formed and able to survive as something more than greedy parasites that devour their strength and grow for nine months to an inconvenient size.

Some mothers, though they're rare, lament the loss of dependency and weep uncontrollably for days or even weeks. But most take a breath and marvel at the newly independent spirit they have struggled to squeeze into the crowded world. Those mothers also weep tears of joy at the unheard voice whispering of the glory that is the child and of the glory that may come as a result of the child. My mother felt the potential glory of my life urgently, and she would not allow anything or anyone to cloud or to alter it.

My mother lived to create in me a love for the things she loved. Books and poetry, our garden, and my father. She did not die until I was fully formed and ready to be released gloriously into the world for the second time. No one else mattered because no one else (not even my father) understood. All things happen for a reason. We are all going to a better place.

But something is set against us.

*

I only had a few minutes to read before my father came into the house after putting the horses away. I knew he wanted to go to town that day. He would not want to keep the red cows any longer than necessary. And he'd want to contact Ed Luke. It was well past the middle of July and the wheat harvest in Garfield County would start no later than the first week in September. We did not have a phone or even a mailbox at our place. We got mail from a box at the post office in town. My mother's natural contrarianism again.

"If someone needs to get in touch with us in a hurry, I guess that means it would be best for us to slow them down a bit, so they can think about what it is they might want from us," she'd say.

I learned to understand that someone's desire to be in touch with our family did not imply a corollary responsibility on our part. We usually checked the mail every two weeks, less often in the winter because the roads often became impassable.

Even as infrequent as it was, mail was an exciting enough prospect for me that I would insist the post office be the first stop we make once we got to town. But my mother believed in patience, which she said is "the art of slowing down." So, we would always check the mail on our way out of town, and she would have time to open and read everything, even the advertisements, on the ride home.

Once a month, along with everyone else in town, we received in the mail a free copy of the Pomeroy's weekly newspaper, *The East Washingtonian.* Since it was late in July, I knew there would be a notice in the paper about enrolling children in school for the coming year. It was also about time for the local school district to send my parents a letter informing them that, by state law, I was required to be enrolled in school. Small town people have always been known for spreading trivial gossip, but when it comes to things that matter, people in towns like Pomeroy tend to be very good at leaving each other alone. So, the matter of my lack of attendance was never pursued.

"Maybe June should be in school," my father would say every year when the letter came. "She might like to be around some other kids. You said yourself she's smarter than most. Heck, they'll even send the bus down to our road. All we'd have to do is get her out there every morning. She's already up before the sun."

My mother always waited to respond. My father's suggestion would usually come as we drove home, so there was time for deliberation. My mother would nod her head two or three times to make sure my father knew she was considering what he had to say. Then she'd turn away and watch the gold-green of the wheat fields glide by outside the truck. Finally, she'd turn to look at me sitting between them with the truck's gear lever rubbing against my left knee.

"I don't know, Jake. When I was in school…"

Isolation was not a unique condition among the farm and ranch children of Garfield County. Most places in those days were far enough from town that kids spent most of their time at home with no neighbors close enough to see. I got along fine with other kids.

Since my father had a valuable talent for building and mechanics and was able to make a difficult colt useful in only two or three days, he frequently got work away from our place, and I'd go along if there were children to play with while he worked. And occasionally, someone would bring a horse or an old tractor to our place for my father to work on. If the farmer had children, he'd bring them along so I'd have playmates at home.

"Sarah, the girl is twelve years old. She ought to be in school."

"I know what she *ought*, Jake. I know. But that doesn't mean I believe what she *ought* is what's *right*."

The idea appealed to me, though I had no experience with school and really had little idea of what went on there. My mother and father would have their brief conversation and then my mother would decide it would be best that I not go, and my father would accept her judgment. And another year would pass.

Then, when I was twelve, we took a summertime trip to town in search of the owner of some wayward red cows. Before that day, my father's skill with wood, engines, or horseflesh was the only reason anyone bothered to find out where we lived.

Chapter 5

June let her father take the horses. She climbed through the rails of the corral and entered the house through the back door and the mudroom. Back in the kitchen, still wearing her hat and heavy coat, she sat at the table and turned to the exact place in her book where she had stopped reading before breakfast. She turned back two pages to re-read the passage about Cupid and his new wife. June had questions. She was determined to understand why Cupid was not allowed to see the face of the god. Was the god vain? Was the princess too young to understand, too frail, insecure, or inconstant? Nothing in the story could be mitigated by either the god's beauty or his proximate power. June thought that strange because she remembered the story of another god who turned himself into a giant swan to subdue a mortal woman who had resisted his advances.

Did she take on his knowledge with his power? Would knowledge put the princess in danger?

She also knew the Revelatory story of the end of the world. Her agile mind began to wrestle with the twin concepts of knowledge and power: the Word of God and the words of the gods. The Bible or the Greeks?

"Most stories go back beyond and through the Bible," her mother had told her.

She wondered. Was the god hovering in the dark afraid he'd turn his sleeping lover into a desperate Helen and nudge the world, therefore, closer to Armageddon?

"Tiger, tiger, burning bright," she said aloud. "The Bible and the Greeks: two ends of the same story."

Sarah was cutting carrots into a large pot sitting on the counter. A bunch of carrots with the crisp green tops still attached lay to the right of the large sink in a pool of garden mud created by dirt that clung to each carrot as it was pulled from the ground. Clear water from the family's well deep beneath the house splashed in a steady stream over each carrot as Sarah scrubbed the dirt away so she could cut them into bite-size chunks. On the other side of the sink, a stack of fat, oddly shaped potatoes covered with the same dirt waited.

June looked up from her book to watch her mother work. She knew there would be stew for dinner, carrots and potatoes, with seasoned chunks of beef or chicken. She was hoping for chicken. The long morning ride with her father left her with no appetite for beef.

Sarah had harvested the carrots and potatoes, while June and Jake retrieved the wayward cattle. Gardening was difficult for Sarah. Her parents had a garden in Bellingham when she was a girl. But it was small and tidy, and the family ate sparingly from the garden every day until their meager harvest was used up. Their garden produce was always supplemented with meat and other fruits and vegetables from the supermarket. Sarah's parents enjoyed talking about their garden when professional friends from the university came to visit. Like so much of what she remembered of her parents' life together, the garden was little more than fodder for conversation, a discussion topic in which an opinion could be expressed and a consensus reached. And it was her father, Sarah recalled, who did most of the gardening.

But if Sarah's garden failed, the family did not eat as well as it might, or financial resources needed elsewhere would have to be used to buy more food during the winter. None of this had ever happened, but it was on Sarah's mind as she cut up the carrots and while the potatoes waited.

The garden had been good this year. A winter's supply of fruits and vegetables—applesauce from the ancient orchard, frozen blackberries from the hillsides to the north, and canned asparagus and tomatoes— were all harvested and prepared at precisely the right time and then stored in the spacious pantry next to the kitchen. When winter came and the garden, the orchard, and the hillsides had yielded the last of their autumn abundance, the family would have boxes and bags of individually wrapped onions, potatoes, apples, and carrots stored in the root cellar beneath the house.

The family had two freezers, one for fruit and vegetables frozen inside sturdy plastic bags and one for meat, including one whole beef that had been born on the ranch. Jake could butcher the cow himself, but Sarah preferred to have the butcher come from town once a year to kill, cut, and wrap the best of the family's yearling steers. The others would be sold at auction. The freezer also contained several chickens. Jake took great pleasure in chopping off their heads each fall so Sarah and June could gut, pluck, and scald them after the headless birds had stopped flopping around in the yard. Once prepared, the chickens were frozen whole.

Most years Jake would shoot a dear or an elk. He took great pride in the gutting, skinning, cutting, and wrapping of any game he was able to shoot. Since he had done the killing, he told June, it was his duty to do the gruesome work of getting the animal ready for the freezer.

Sarah had never been physically strong, so the garden was arduous work. But so was perfecting the soul, and she had prodigious strength in that area. The garden was the soul of the family's larder, so she worked deliberately at both: cultivating the land and cultivating grace with equal resolve. The process of tilling the soil, planting, weeding, and harvesting began as soon as the snow began to disappear in early March and continued until the snow returned in November. Sarah loved the feel of her own vegetables in her own hands as she scrubbed off her own dirt to feed her own family. She loved the enormous disparity between the purpose of her family's garden and the organic designs of her parents. As she scrubbed and cut up the last of the carrots, it occurred to her that these carrots had been out of the ground for less than an hour. The remarkable fact that her family's dinner had traveled less than a hundred feet to reach her kitchen made her smile and then laugh.

"What is it?" June asked. "What's so funny?"

"These carrots and potatoes were in the ground in our own garden just this morning. Isn't that remarkable?"

"I know where they came from. It's not remarkable at all. It's where they always come from."

Sarah laughed again. For June, the source of the family's vegetables wasn't remarkable in any way. She plopped the last of the carrots into the cook pot. She turned away from the sink and strode across the room to where June sat reading the passage about the faceless god and her uncertain lover for the third time. She stood directly behind the girl and kissed her lightly on top of the head.

"June, honey. I'm so glad you do not understand."

*

Sarah was heading back toward the sink when Jake came through the back door and saw his wife working.

"You've been in the garden," he said. "We're having soup, ain't we?"

"More like stew, I think. I'll put onions in with the potatoes and carrots and meat when we get back from town."

"Well, we need to get goin' then. June, get in the truck. You can take your book and read on the way in. Sarah, get your coat. It's likely to be cold by the time we get back."

"Jake, neither you nor that girl is going to town until you clean yourselves up. It's bad enough some people in town think we're nothing but ignorant mountain trash. You and June clean up and put on something besides those work clothes. You were chasing cattle all morning so I'm certain you smell bad as well."

Jake sighed and stared at his wife. She stared back. He thought about trying to convince her that it was getting late.

"June, honey," he said with a smirk. "Go on upstairs and get cleaned up and dressed for town. Your momma thinks we look trashy and poor."

She closed her book and headed upstairs. He waited for the girl to leave the room before he approached Sarah from the back and put his arms around her waist. He pulled her away from the sink and slid his hand under the bottom of his wife's homemade blouse and gently rubbed the warm skin of her stomach. He'd noticed that her skin had begun to feel thinner, stretched tight and dry over the narrow muscles of her abdomen and hips, but he said nothing about it.

"You know, just about everyone in town today will of come in off the farm or ranch. We ain't gonna be outta place in our work clothes."

"You do what you want," she said as she pushed his hand away. "But our daughter is going to be clean and presentable. We live out here in the mountains, but I don't want people to think June is common or low."

"There's not much common about that girl. I'll be ready in fifteen minutes."

He went up the stairs to shower, shave, and dress while she scrubbed and cut up the potatoes and added beef stew meat to the pot. She put the pot on the stove and adjusted the burner so the meat and the vegetables would simmer until they came home later in the afternoon.

June came downstairs washed, combed, and dressed in a straight cotton dress with tiny frogs printed on the fabric. She sat at the kitchen table reading about the goddess and her lover until her parents were ready to leave.

It was well after noon by the time they made their way from the ranch to the blacktop twelve miles away. Sarah packed sandwiches and apples for the forty-minute journey to Pomeroy. The old silver-and-black pickup was dented and peeling. It rattled in the ruts of the gravel road before it reached the paved highway. Jake was fond of driving faster than Sarah liked, and June was exhilarated when her father pushed the old truck past sixty when they reached the paved road.

Travelers on Highway 12 who reached Pomeroy from the east or the west were surprised when the speed limit slowed to thirty miles per hour for two miles through town. The hundred-year-old courthouse was in nearly pristine condition, and enough of the rest of "downtown" Pomeroy had resisted the temptation to modernize, or in some cases, to even repair itself, so people passing through got a four-minute history lesson. The town sat on the floor of a narrow valley with Pataha Creek crawling along the bottom during the spring and autumn months. The creek was dry or nearly dry during the summer and much of the winter. Most of the town was jammed onto the floor of the valley between steep hillsides. To the north rolled the endless wheat fields of the Palouse. The lush green winter wheat would gradually ripen to a rich brown as summer progressed and then shimmer golden in early autumn. Throughout the year, graceful arcs of unplanted ground striped the fields. Broad, bare belts of dark summer fallow protected the fecundity of the rich soil.

The wheat country to the south of town rolled more gently than the steep Palouse Hills to the north, even flattening out briefly before the cultivated land gave way to the wilderness of the Blue Mountain. The most prominent geological feature of the Blue Mountains in Garfield County was a rugged mass of granite appropriately called "Mount Misery." Except for a handful of small ranches like the one inhabited by June and her family, the Blue Mountains south of Pomeroy were mostly inaccessible, even uninhabitable.

But Pomeroy was a cozy community. Hospitality came second nature to people who work the land. In the old days, when farmers and ranchers ventured into town once or twice a year, at a time when a good man with a patient wife could live his entire life and never travel farther than the thirty miles to Clarkston or Dayton, strangers were welcomed for the news they brought from the outside world. Visitors were still welcome, though people had grown more wary, because while Pomeroy had remained much the same, the outside world had changed.

Traveling to Pomeroy from the south, the town was not apparent until the traveler was well inside the city limits. The mountains gave way reluctantly to fifteen miles of wheat. The wheat fields finally gave way to a two-mile glide down through a broad canyon and into town.

Jake slowed the truck when they reached the city limits. When he reached Highway 12, which doubled as the main street of the town, he turned right and drove slowly past the ancient courthouse. Halfway through town, he pulled up in front of the feed store and parked his truck. Across the street was Sarah and June's destination, a general store that doubled as the town's hardware and dry goods supplier, Jake would ask about the red cows at the feed store.

He had never really felt at home until he and Sarah settled down on her family's ancestral ranch in the Blue Mountains. He could stay on the ranch for months at a time and never feel the need to go to town. He was a solitary man who lacked the natural need to "herd up" with other people.

He was born in Eastern Washington, on the far northern rim of the state near the Canadian border. His parents were members of a single-minded colony of "mountain folk," the children and grandchildren of sharecroppers driven from the Deep South by drought and privation in the 1930s. In the years following the Depression, a close settlement of former Southerners set up more than two dozen hand-to-mouth households in the rugged mountains around Oroville. Jake went to school in Oroville off and on, but formal learning was not a priority among some of the hill people. When Jake was needed at home, he stayed home. His father was a sour man who the locals generally referred to as "no count," an assessment which many of the hill people tended to agree with. Unlike most families in the mountains, the union between his father and his illiterate mother produced only a single child. That fact was clear evidence in the scattered community of Jake's father's unwillingness to behave responsibly. Large families meant more hands, and more hands in the days before nutrition programs and welfare payments meant a greater chance of survival. Jake was his parents' only offspring, and since his father had an aversion to work, the family's lot was harder than most.

He wasn't an ambitious boy. It would've been easy for him to simply settle into the indigent ways of his father, save for two things. He was present at school just often enough through the eighth grade that he learned to read, write, and count. His parents sent him to school as soon as he was old enough, mostly so they wouldn't have to look after him. He was able to get to school only because of his maternal grandfather, a man keenly disappointed that his youngest daughter's choice of a mate was determined by a sudden pregnancy at fourteen. Jubal Allen was named for a Confederate hero in the Civil War and was considered something of a leader among the mountain folk, because he worked often enough and hard enough to create a modest amount of surplus income, some of which he squandered on his daughter and invested in Jake. His cabin in the mountains had a sound roof and a good wood floor. His wife and six children lacked the eternally hungry countenance that made the mountain folk easy to identify when they were in town.

Jubal even had a truck that ran. When the weather permitted in the fall or in the spring, he would arrive at his daughter's rickety shack early every morning and drive Jake to school. Snow made it treacherous for many of the mountain people to get to town during the hard winter months, so Jake simply did not go to school during the winter. At other times of the year, his father spitefully refused to allow the boy to go to school, insisting disingenuously he was needed at home. Jake's father had not attended school beyond the third grade, and Jubal was deeply ashamed that Jake's mother, his own daughter, could not read or write.

If Jake had shown more promise, school officials would have made arrangements to either get him to school during the winter months or to make sure the work he needed to keep up was available to him at home. Such had been the case for three of Jubal's older children.

Jake's schooling became a matter of bitter contention between Jubal and his son-in-law, but Jake was not intelligent in the school sense and was content to attend school when his grandfather insisted or not attend when the elements or his father prevented him.

The boy's minimal literacy aside, Jubal's greater gift to Jake was knowledge gleaned and lessons learned during the long days of the mountain summer. From the depths of the Depression, Jubal had brought prodigious practical skill. He could build a house from the materials provided by the mountains; he could provide food to feed his large family from the meager bounty of the forest and the earth. He knew the ins and outs of engines. He had an uncompromising way with animals, especially horses, which was a skill that, like Jake years later, would make him a valuable asset to the area's cattle ranchers. Jake learned all these things from his grandfather, never knowing that his grandfather's legacy and an unknown and innate capacity for survival would prove in time to be far more valuable than anything he would learn at school.

Chapter 6

My mother had a peculiar habit. When the weather was warm enough, and sometimes even when it wasn't, she would walk alone along the creek that flowed through our property until she arrived at the same secluded spot. There she would take off all her clothes except for a pair of light canvas shoes. She would place the clothes in a neat pile and sit down on them at the edge of the creek. In the summer when the weather was especially warm, she would find a deep spot and wade into the running water to bathe herself all over. At other times she would leave her clothes in the neat pile and walk along the edge of the creek or up the slope and wander among the sparse underbrush with only those canvas shoes for protection.

She didn't do this in secret, and my mother was no exhibitionist. She made no attempt to hide this practice from me or from my father, though I know he was never…comfortable with it. And, like so many of my childhood memories, this practice did not seem strange to me at all. Only much later did I learn from others that taking your clothes off in the forest might be strange, so I never wondered about the propriety of this practice.

On the day before my father and I rode after the red cows and the three of us rode in the truck to Pomeroy, my mother came back from a walk in the woods with wet shoes, and I knew what she'd been doing.

As I almost always did when she returned from her walks, I followed her upstairs to the one room in the house she claimed for herself. I knew she would undress again and replace the light dress she had worn on her walk with denim pants and a man-style button-up shirt. My mother was small, but she never looked frail unless she was completely naked, as if her clothes created the illusion that she was stronger than she was. Her apparent physicality, which was necessary to thrive on our remote ranch, seemed to evaporate when she undressed. I watched as she stretched and rubbed her lower back. Her skin was beginning to develop an ethereal, almost translucent quality. I watched until she was dressed and appeared strong again.

"Mom, why do you take your clothes off when you go walking?"

She never failed, out of shame, conceit, or misgiving, to answer whenever I asked a question…on any subject. The question had occurred to me, so she assumed I was grown up enough to hear the answer, unadorned by parental subtlety or age-appropriate nicety.

"Things are seldom what they appear," she told me. And I thought some more about what seemed to be the gradual and obvious diminishment of her body. "And people are never who they appear to be. Neither you nor I nor your father can see the truth of a thing. Oh, we can recognize a thing's usefulness or know when it's a threat, but we're often not able to see its good nature. And people put on garments and masks every day, hoping to keep their own good nature from each other and even from themselves."

I was left to suppose that my mother's habit of periodic, solitary nakedness had something to do with revealing to herself—as there was never anyone else present—who she really was, or at least who she really might have been.

"Self-deceit is the greatest sin," she said. "And humility, seeing ourselves for what we really are, our own good nature, does not come naturally."

Our ranch house in the Blue Mountains was the only home I had ever known. My mother's singular inclinations were perfectly normal in the remote world I inhabited during the first twelve years of my life. I didn't realize until later that mine was a real life of wonderment, a genuine fantasy created for me by my mother and guarded by my father. I was unaware that my life was in any significant way different from my infrequent playmates, but, like the curious lover of the faceless god in the myth, my innocence was about to be stripped away.

"Make-believe is for books," my mother said. "We must make our own lives real."

When we arrived in Pomeroy that day, my father parked the truck in front of the general store so my mother and I wouldn't have to cross the street. He waited until we were out of the truck and watched frowning as we entered the store. I remember it crossed my mind that he must also be aware of the change in my mother's appearance. How could he not be? Once we were inside, I turned and watched through the large window as my father left the truck and crossed the street to the feed store. My mother was already in the back rummaging through bolts of fabric by the time I turned to follow her.

"We need to find something stout and warm so we can make you some new clothes for the winter," she said as I walked up to her. "And by spring you'll be too big to wear any of the clothes you're wearing now."

"Won't you need new clothes too?"

"My clothes are fine. I'll just take some things in."

My mother's words struck like a thunderbolt in the dark, a flash of illumination igniting the inferno that devastates the countryside. Elegance and calamity inhabiting the same moment. Was I increasing, or was the scope and scale of my life growing while hers was receding? Was I the cause of her disappearance? The fearful symmetry of that possibility made my heart ache, and I thought again about the goddess and her lover.

Chapter 7

Jake watched Sarah and June enter the general store and then sat in the truck. Like his daughter, he was aware that Sarah was losing weight fast. Before they left the ranch, he asked her to visit Pomeroy's small hospital and clinic while they were in town. But she refused. Sarah habitually corrected her husband when he "misspoke."

"I'm declining to see a doctor, I'm not refusing," she told him. "If they think there's anything wrong, they'll just send me down to Lewiston to see another doctor who'll tell me I'm fine or that I'm not. If I'm fine, we'd have wasted a trip. If I'm not, there won't be much they can do that matters in the long run. So, no hospital and no doctor."

Jake would not often argue with his wife. He didn't believe her to be stubborn. It was more that she thought about things a step or two beyond where his more practical mind stopped. Still, as he sat in the truck, he wondered what he might do to change her mind.

While he thought, a large truck and trailer rig rumbled by on the street. Its diesel engine labored to slow down under the legal weight of the town's thirty-mile-per-hour speed limit. Nothing occurred to him, so he got out of the pickup and crossed the street to the feed store. When he reached the other side, a second big rig decelerated clumsily. The noise from the truck's heavy brakes and the grinding of gears was deafening while the driver double-clutched down to the legal limit. Jake stopped on the sidewalk and turned to see that the truck driver had waited too long to slow down. A green-and-white police car with its red and blue lights flashing eased itself out of the next side street and pulled in behind the truck.

Crime had never been much of a problem in Pomeroy. The most frequent violation of the local codes was speeding through town. The speed limit on Highway 12 was sixty miles per hour to the east and west of the city limits, and drivers, especially truckers, had a hard time adjusting to half that speed when they reached the town. These frequent extra-legal incidents were managed by the two-man Garfield County Sheriff's Department with a polite warning for locals and with stiff fines or a night in jail for out-of-towners and habitually offending truckers.

Highway 12 was the only convenient access route from the Snake River port at Lewiston, Idaho to Interstate 84, which ran all the way from Hermiston, Oregon to Portland to the west and to Boise and Salt Lake City to the southeast. Truckers in a hurry learned quickly that Pomeroy's thirty-mile-per-hour limit did not mean thirty-one miles per hour. Jake watched with a shake of his head as another truck driver was about to have his schedule and bank account disrupted by inattention to or a lack of awareness of Garfield County's strict traffic laws.

The truck driver's innocent carelessness had distracted Jake, but when he turned back toward the street, he saw June watching him through the big windows of the general store. He raised his hand to wave at the girl. She turned her head away as if indicating the presence of her mother at the rear of the store. He did not lower his hand until she turned her attention back to him. When the girl caught his gaze, he nodded once and entered the feed store.

Except for its intolerance of outsiders who violate the traffic laws, the people of Pomeroy were fond of leaving each other alone. They were also adept, when necessity required, at taking care of each other. During the years when June was growing up on the ranch, the county did not have a relief or welfare office, but no one could ever remember anyone in the county going hungry or passing a nasty Palouse winter without a heavy coat. Sarah gathered up the homemade clothes that June outgrew every year, packed them in a box, and gave instructions to Jake to deliver the old clothes to Elsie Luke when he went to work for her husband, Ed, each fall. Sarah described Elsie affectionately as "Pomeroy's official full-time busybody."

Sarah did not involve herself in community projects, but she was opposed to waste. Elsie knew every child in the Pomeroy schools, she knew which families on which farms were suffering most in hard times, and she had the phone number and was on a first-name basis with every clergyman's wife in town. Sarah could depend on Elsie to find someone who would put June's well-made hand-me-downs to good use and then later pass the clothes on to someone else.

Jake was hoping to find Ed in the feed store because he needed to talk about when the harvest would start, and if anyone knew anything about the red cows, it would be Ed. Sarah also hoped Ed was in town because that meant Elsie would be shopping in the general store while her husband hung around the feed store talking about beef prices, moisture, and the protein content of that year's wheat. Elsie was the closest thing Sarah had to a friend. She was several years older than Sarah and had lived in Pomeroy all her life. She spent twelve years in the Pomeroy schools sharing a classroom with Ed Luke the entire time. There were twenty-five kids who started the first grade in Pomeroy with Ed and Elsie, and seventeen of the same kids walked across the makeshift stage in the gym at high school graduation. Ed and Elsie had known each other even longer. They were children of the two most successful growers in the county, born on adjoining wheat and cattle ranches. Ed's proposal to Elsie on graduation night merely formalized a foregone conclusion, and they were married four years later when he returned to Pomeroy, clutching a degree in economics from the University of Idaho up in Moscow.

He began running the family's ranch immediately, and when Elsie's parents retired ten years later, their sizeable spread was combined with his parents' land to form one of the largest wheat and cattle operations in eastern Washington. In the agriculture business, rain or lack of rain, snow or lack of snow, or beef prices in Argentina, or diminished demand in Japan, or a cattle disease scare in Canada can mean financial disaster for small operators. Size increases the margin for error, so the consolidation of Ed and Elsie's family holdings was a matter of practicality, as if two enormous fiefs had been ceded by wealthy vassals to celebrate and formalize the confluence of prominent bloodlines. The enlarged Luke farm was big enough to make a lot of money during those rare years when the mysterious forces of the agricultural cosmos lined up to enhance the farmers' economic situation. Careful husbandry of those precious surplus resources made it possible for Ed's ranch to survive when the ruthless calculus of international markets and the perversity of the elements forced their smaller neighbors into foreclosure.

Elsie was much more than a farmer's wife. She was the matriarch of the largest holding in the county. She had been brought up to understand without question or reservation her inherited responsibility, to maintain the traditional social and cultural fabric of the county, which came with her exalted position. Family history could be as solid in the Palouse as the bedrock geology of the ancient hills, and husbanding local tradition could be as vital to the county's survival as plowing, planting, and harvesting in the correct sequence and at the proper time. She knew without being told that she and Ed were graced with blessings that were denied to many of their neighbors. A carefully cultivated sense of duty demanded constant repayment of that grace, an ongoing sharing of the cosmic wealth. She was on the school board, the park board, and the library board, and she was the president of the County Fair Association. And she loved books, and she read them, which was how she and Sarah had become friends.

When Jake entered the feed store, a sizable concentration of farmers and ranchers were clustered around a cold wood stove in a corner away from the door. The men were drinking coffee and loudly sharing opinions on everything from the weather to the price of diesel. The wood-stove assembly stopped talking for a moment to see who had come in, nodded a polite greeting to Jake, and then resumed their conversation. He did not join the group, but instead queried the store's owner, Ralph Parsons, an intensely quiet man who was supporting his considerable bulk with his elbows on the counter trying to listen in to the conversation.

"Ed Luke been in today?" Jake asked.

"He's right over there," Ralph said, nodding in the direction of a small stack of bulky feed sacks on the opposite side of the large room. Ralph did not waste floor space with crowded rows of merchandise displays. Everyone knew he would have anything almost anyone would need at almost any time, so he kept the bulk of his stock in a large warehouse in the back of the building or in a large lot on the edge of town across the highway from the grain elevator. He'd never been a farmer or rancher himself, but he reasoned that men who spent their entire working lives outdoors did not want to feel cramped when they came into town. So, there was plenty of room to congregate inside the store.

The stack of feed sacks was just the right height to allow Ed to lean back and rest his hips against the top sack. When local people talked about Ed Luke and his position in the county, outsiders usually assumed he would be a very large man with a booming voice and a commanding presence, but he wasn't. Barely five foot eight, he had trouble keeping his denim work jeans on his hips, even in middle age. When he came to town, Ed was showered and clean shaven, and his plain-colored clothes were nearly new. His white straw cowboy hat was pushed back on his head and his legs were crossed so his deeply polished, sharp-toed boots would not scuff each other.

"Thanks," Jake said as he turned away from the counter.

Ed stood up straight when he approached.

"How you doin'?" he said, extending his right hand. "How're Sarah and that little girl getting' along?"

Jake took his hand and gripped it lightly. Even though he and Ed were quite obviously on opposite rungs of the county's social and economic ladder, Ed didn't make him feel like he had to prove himself with a vice-like handshake. Ed knew the difference between wealth and worth, and Jake's skill with livestock and his dexterity with machinery made him worthy. He would've hired Jake as a full-time hand and even provided a place for his family if Sarah would've allowed it.

"Everyone's fine, Ed. Thanks for askin'. I got coupla things I'd like to speak with you about, though."

"I figured you'd be around. It's about that time of the year, isn't it? Well, we'll be starting the harvest a little early, about the first week in September. I'd appreciate it if you could move onto our place about a week before that. I don't want any glitches once we start up the combines and some of the equipment may need work done before we start."

"I wonder if I might drive up to your place every day, this year. Sarah don't seem quite…well …that is, I don't want to be away from her and June any more than I have to."

"It'll take you more than an hour to drive up to my place, not to mention the cost of fuel."

"I know, but I really don't think I should be gone that much right now."

Ed thought about what Jake had said. Sarah had never objected to the time her husband spent on his ranch every fall. She and June always managed their place fine while he was gone.

"Tell you what, we'll clean out that little house at the back of our home place, and you can bring June and Sarah along with you."

"I don't know, Ed we got stock to look after, and…"

Ed knew he had spoken too quickly. As soon as Jake and Sarah moved into the county, many people in town thought the family was going to be a charity case. He knew Sarah didn't care much what anyone thought, but Jake could get touchy when he believed someone thought he couldn't provide for his family.

"What have you got?" Ed said. "That old bull and three or four cow-calf pairs?"

"We got eight pairs," he said in protest. "And the horses."

Ed slapped him hard on the right shoulder and left his hand in place to make sure he had Jake's attention. "You can turn your horses and that bull out with the cows. There's plenty of feed in your hills this time of year. It's not necessary, but you can go home on Sundays to check on 'em if you need to.

"And I'll pick up a lotta points with Elsie when I tell her I convinced you to bring Sarah to our place. And my brother will be there the whole time with his kids. He's gotta boy a little older than June, I think, and a girl a year or two younger.

"And I'll make sure everyone in this county and the next one knows that the three of you are earning your keep while you're on my place."

"Ah, Ed, that ain't it."

"The hell it isn't. I was sayin' to Elsie just the other day, 'How did a man as stubborn as Jake ever end up with a woman like Sarah, with her feet planted firm like right down into the ground?'"

"OK, Ed. I'll talk to Sarah."

The two men stood silently for a long moment. Jake wanted to ask him about the extra cows, but he could sense Ed had something else to say, so he didn't press. He knew that Ed was measuring his words, so he waited.

"There's one more thing, Jake," he said. "Elsie come home from the school board meeting the other night…"

For Jake and Sarah, the school board was the one local institution they had stubbornly avoided any contact with, so he tried to steer the conversation in a different direction.

"Wait, Ed. Before I forget. I got some extra cows at my place. Six Herefords that June and me brought up from one of our south-end pastures down on the border. They ain't mine, and I wonder if anyone in town knows anything about 'em."

"I'll ask around and make a couple of calls to folks I know down that way, but, Jake, I got to tell you what Elsie said."

He didn't want to hear what Elsie said, but courtesy and respect demanded that he at least let Ed have his say.

"There was a fella from Olympia, from the state school board, or whatever it is over there. He's makin' the rounds of all these small towns to be sure everyone knows the law about kids being in school. And he said if the school board knows of any kids who aren't then they got to get those kids rounded up and in school, even if it means gettin' the sheriff involved."

"What are you sayin'?"

"Someone mentioned June to the state guy after the meeting and said you and Sarah have to put her in school. It's the law."

He didn't say anything. He removed his hat and ran his fingers through his hair, then replaced his hat and rubbed both sides of his face with his fingertips.

"We talk about it every year. But Sarah is pretty set against it. She and June…they study things I don't know nothin' about."

"That girl of yours can't live down there on that ranch for her whole life."

"Sarah says she can. Says it would be good if June lived her whole life down there. I just don't know. I guess me and Sarah can talk about it again."

Now it was Ed who said nothing. He and Elsie both felt tender toward Jake and his family. He'd known of one or two other families who did not want their kids in school. But they always gave in. If the sheriff's gentle explanation of the legal consequences wasn't convincing, then a visit from a stern woman from Child Protective Services in Clarkston usually was. In one case a family went so far as to move out of the county entirely.

But Ed also knew there was something about June that set her apart from those other kids. Something Elsie had commented on once.

"You know, Ed," Elsie said. "Every time Sarah and I talk about a book, after a few minutes June jumps right into the conversation."

"She probably doesn't get that many people to talk to down there on that ranch. I'm sure she doesn't mean to be impolite."

"No, that's not it. June's already read whatever book we're talking about. The child is twelve years old, and she's read everything I've read in my entire life. She's a wonder."

Jake started to walk away.

"Wait," Ed said. "The sheriff was at that school board meeting. Elsie said he told the guy from the state board that it wouldn't do any good for him to visit with you and Sarah. He said that as far as he could tell, June was just about the smartest youngster in the county. And since she hadn't spent so much as a single day in a school room, he didn't see how it would make any difference if she was in school or not."

Jake thought about the sheriff pulling over the speeding big rig a few minutes earlier. "I always liked the way Tom goes about his work," he said. "I'll thank him when I see him."

"That wasn't the end of it," Ed said. "When the sheriff got done talkin', the man from the state asked if he was refusing to do his duty. The sheriff said he didn't see how it was his duty to cause trouble for people who weren't doin' anyone any harm.

"Then, Elsie said, the man from the state told the sheriff, 'They're harming that child' and if the sheriff would not do what's necessary to get June into school, the state board would file a neglect complaint with CPS. When Elsie tried to tell him June was looked after as well as any child in the county, he told her the state has the authority to take June from you and Sarah and put her into school."

Jake was silent for a long time. He felt his fist begin to clench and the tension ran up his forearms into his shoulders. He relaxed and listened while Ed continued.

"I just thought you and Sarah should know what might happen if June doesn't go to school."

"Where's Elsie now?"

"She's across the street. I imagine she's tellin' Sarah the same story. What are you going to do?"

"I'm going to get my wife and my child and go home. I don't think anyone better come after us."

Chapter 8

My mother insisted on strict definitions. Words and deeds had precise meanings, and she did not believe in uncertainty. And I never knew my mother to need anyone. She told my father once that she loved him without condition and without reservation but need implies compulsion and assigns to another an expectation that cannot reasonably be met.

"And," she said to me. "Would it be fair to your father if I were to make him responsible for my happiness, or for yours? He has a life to live too."

Still, if she ever came close to needing anyone, it would've been Elsie Luke. Elsie was the woman my mother might've become if her early circumstances had been different. When Elsie said I needed to "get an education," her comment must've nudged my mother away from her comfortable certainty. I know this because for the first time, I was uncertain about the course my mother was setting for me. If Elsie believed I should be in school, then maybe…

Until a certain age, all children believe their parents are infallible and, if not omniscient, sincere. Until that afternoon in the general store, I'd no experience to suggest my mother would ever make a poor decision. I was twelve years old and had never doubted her, had never seen my father press her on any issue beyond the point of making his own opinion known to her. I never, in any way, thought of my father as weak. In fact, his silent acknowledgement and acceptance of my mother's authority on matters of my intellectual and spiritual upbringing was evidence then and is proof now of his uncompromising wisdom.

My father strode through the door of the general store and stopped. He could see my mother at the back of the store listening while Elsie talked. Elsie was much shorter than my mother, so she had to reach up to grasp her left arm near the shoulder, as if to keep her from running away. My father could not see me because I was standing behind a tall display filled with neatly folded plain-colored work shirts on one side and heavy blue denim pants on the other. He stepped away from the door to a spot where he could watch.

I knew what they were talking about. I can remember gentler versions of the same argument from Elsie over the years, but this time her tone was much more urgent. A firm and determined insistence had replaced her normal quiet encouragement. I knew what my mother would say, so I watched my father. He leaned against the wall calmly and took off his hat and held it in both hands at his waist. I remember seeing his chest rise and fall slowly. He would not speak of the matter of my schooling until we were in the truck, maybe not until we were home.

"This is serious, Sarah," Elsie said. "The state is serious. They will find out that June has never been in school, they will come to your pace, and they will..."

My mother held up her right hand. "I know. But I'm serious too. June is *my* child. She does not belong to the state."

"But the law, Sarah, the law—"

"The *law* is wrong. Wrong."

Elsie released my mother's arm and shook her head. "Sarah, I love you like a sister. I couldn't love June more if she were my own child. But that girl needs an education. I understand how you and Jake want to live. But there are rules. Sarah, honey, there are times when I envy you. But they will force you to put June in school. They could even take her away from you. Please, it's only school."

My mother folded her hands, raised them prayerfully to her chin, and nodded her head. I looked at my father and could see he'd stepped away from the wall and put his hat back on.

"You're right, Elsie. It is *only* school."

My mother turned away from Elsie, and my father opened the door and waited until she went through. I stepped out from behind the display of pants and shirts. He nodded at me and indicated with his chin that I should follow. Elsie placed her hand on my shoulder and applied a very small amount of gentle pressure. I smiled up at her.

"June, darlin', what's going to become of you? What's going to become of all this?"

I thought of the god without a face, and I thought of his lover groping in the dark for something she could never fully possess. I thought of what my mother said about the Bible and all the old stories. I looked around the general store at all the things people could buy, needful things, things they could have if they would just pay the price.

I took Elsie's hand away from my shoulder and held it in mine, my momentary doubt about my mother's infallibility and my father's wisdom gone.

"Ma'am, I'm going to go home now."

"I'll pray for you, child."

"My mother believes in prayer."

"When we pray to have our needs met, all our prayers are answered," my mother told me once. "All our needs are guaranteed, but none of our desires. June, God will see to our needs. Our desires are up to us."

I let go of Elsie's hand and started toward the door after my parents, desiring nothing more than for my family to remain whole even though I was not, at that time, permitted to know what that meant.

"Tell your momma I'll see her soon."

"I will. But she already knows that."

Chapter 9

Sarah was already in the truck, but she was sitting in June's accustomed place in the center next to her husband. June paused before getting in, but when Sarah did not move, the girl got into her mother's spot next to the passenger side door. Jake put the truck in reverse and then waited for another big rig to lug by before he backed out and headed east away from the center of town. At the grain elevator, he turned right and followed the highway up the narrow canyon toward the south end of the county. June leaned back into the old truck's worn seat and opened her book.

Jake was worried.

"Sarah, we've got to decide what to do. Ed said they…"

Sarah was turned halfway toward the passenger side of the truck so her legs would not be in the way of the gear lever. She leaned lightly against his shoulder and looked over the top of June's head at the walls of the canyon. She said nothing but continued to stare out the window until the truck reached the top of the long grade. When the roadway emerged from the canyon and the vast expanse of gold-green wheat stretched out in front of the truck, she spoke.

"We're going to go home. Our life has nothing to do with what Ed and Elsie said. Our life has nothing to do with anything going on in town."

He continued the drive home at a steady, unhurried speed. June stared at the pages of her book, alternately focusing on the story of the princess in the dark and letting her mind wander to what her mother must be thinking. She knew the children she shared rare playtime with were either compliantly ambivalent or aggressively unenthusiastic about school.

She was curious about what she might learn in school that she had not learned at home or that she didn't know already. She shared Sarah's gift for easily acquiring mathematics and her mother's love of books. The girl had discovered as she grew and became stronger, the manual skills that made her father so valuable to Ed Luke were also easily within her apprehension. But in almost all other particulars she was a remarkably uncurious child. She had an anomalous disinterest in both the details of the lives of other families and the specific nature of the outside world. She had seen homes in town and on other ranches that were grander than the utilitarian, century-old structure she shared with her mother and father, but she knew of no family in town or in the country who, according to the singular set of criteria set by her mother, actually lived any better than they did. The family's rigorous life in the Blue Mountains was not in any way the serene country life covetously imagined by city dwellers, but it was unhurried and quiet. Even at twelve, June had a sense that such was not the case for any other family she knew about. She also had a sense acquired, like everything else, as a steady certainty expressed by her mother, that school might be the reason for at least some of the disquiet she sensed in other families.

Elsie had said she needed an education, but did not say for what. The only time June had heard either of her parents say anything about "education" in the way Elsie meant it was when her father told her he had "escaped" school when Sarah made him realize his genius for practical things was more valuable than anything he had failed to learn in school.

Sarah's parents' approach to education was to insist their daughter shine bright enough to reflect a favorable light upon them. Schooling's end was the attainment of status, the assignment of a number that would place Sarah and, by implication, her mother and father in an exalted position among the academic literati. They believed the power of academic achievement was much more than simply redemptive. An apotheosis was possible, the elevation of a learned elect to the status of gods.

Sarah had no quarrel with her parents' assumption at first. But gradually, and inevitably, she began to recognize that her substantial intellect was being molded to form a life that would not be her own. One day after reaching that conclusion, she asked her mother, "If not my life, whose?" Sarah's mother opened her mouth to answer, and, finding nothing to say that would satisfy the girl, frowned and shook her head.

The truck had reached the end of the blacktop at a gentle left-hand curve in the road. Jake decelerated slowly to keep the rear wheels from sliding in the gravel. Sarah sat up in the seat and leaned away from her husband. She put her left hand on his knee and her right arm on the back of the seat and around June's shoulders.

"June, do you *want* to…No. Do you *think* you should go to school?"

The question caught Jake off guard, and he glanced over quickly to see June's reaction. The girl was still staring at the pages of her book, but he couldn't tell if she was reading. She did not answer her mother's question immediately. After a long silence, she closed her book and looked out the passenger side window of the truck as the last of the wheat fields gave way to the Blue Mountain forest.

"June?" he said. But Sarah squeezed his leg to let him know that no parental admonition was necessary. He glanced sideways at his wife, and she shook her head slightly and mouthed the word "wait" to indicate he should say nothing. June's eyes returned to the book on her lap. Had she become the princess in the dark, co-joined with a god she was not privileged to see in daylight?

"I don't know. It's hard to tell. Isn't it, Mom? You said the stories are not true, but that the truth is in them. Didn't you say that? When the princess sees the god, he is beautiful. But she can't handle it. Once she knows what he looks like, and he finds out, she is sent away. Maybe not knowing is better, for now. No. I don't want to go to school."

The truck continued toward the narrow dirt track that would lead the family home. Jake slowed a long way from the track and then turned carefully off the gravel road. The truck crawled along for another mile. Just as it labored over the low ridge that shielded their home place from the outside world, June opened her book again and sat it unread on her lap.

"There's stew for supper," Sarah said.

"Ed wants us all to come and stay at his place during harvest," he said.

Sarah rubbed her upper arms. Her fingertips reached nearly to the bone. She closed her eyes and breathed until the truck rolled through the gate and stopped in front of the house.

"That's very kind of Ed. If you must go, then go. But June won't be safe there."

Chapter 10

The ingredients were already in place, so school was only the catalyst. I still don't think it was the education I might have received that made my mother uneasy. It was the compulsory nature of public school, the assumption she would bend once the legal and social consequences were spelled out. My mother's body had begun to show its frailty that summer, but as her physical life waned, something deeper and firmer quickened.

I think most people have a backlog of tenderly ambivalent memories of their parents. They have images of particular incidents that shape their understanding of the people most responsible for the adults they will become.

Since leaving our mountain home, I've noticed that parents often take too much credit for their children when they succeed and are just as often assigned too much blame when they fail. People remember fondly a father who beamed with pride over a well-thrown ball, then brood when that same father misses the last game of the season. Childhood is a cluster of infrequent snapshots tucked away in an immaterial cerebral catalogue, each page devoted to a particular mood or a specific emotion.

I think this is typical.

But I have no such particular memories of my mother. The time we had together stretches before me in an unbroken array with her alone at the beginning and myself fully formed and finished by age twelve at the end. In the discreet memories I do have, my mother is pointing out a vivid image in a book or explaining the usefulness of a plant in the woods or digging in the garden or praying naked in the forest. If what others have told me is true, many lives are defined by poetic images of concentrated experience separated by intermittent spaces of time alone. But after many years of ordering and cataloguing my childhood memories, I have come to view my own life with my mother in epic terms, one verse rolling seamlessly day by day into another until I am the blind lover reaching out in the dark to a jealous god raging on the mountain.

I need to stop.

The visions come too fast.

They overlap and I become confused.

I do not believe my mother ever harbored any covert affection for the human race. She was a great believer in individual human beings, but she did not trust groups or institutions. In her last days she resisted with all her diminishing power any attenuation of my life in the service of some unspecified and indistinct greater good.

I wonder how my memories would now align if I'd told my mother I wanted to go to school. In my preadolescent mind, the question of school really did not seem that important. I was healthy and happy, and I had a book in my lap. I really liked being at home with both of my parents. I loved our life, and I thought everyone in our narrow acquaintance lived in a similar manner. I am certain now it was inevitable change and not *formal* schooling that I wished to hold at a safe distance. The adjustment in our family life that school required would be unwelcome. For my mother, who was adept at adjustment, it was *requirement*, the claim of essentiality, the naked compulsion, and the legal demand on our family's time and way of living she objected to.

For me, like Elsie, "it was only school." But for my mother it was much more. There was a sacred principle involved, though I was not aware of the principle at the time.

When outsiders consider the way we lived, an essential misunderstanding is almost guaranteed. A good friend of Elsie's, a woman who had left Pomeroy after she was married, once commented to my mother, as I stood silently listening in the background, that it must be satisfying to live off the land and to grow our own food.

"I wish I had your courage," she said. "To leave the city and get back to nature. It must be very rewarding."

The woman was well dressed. Her clothes fit but had a calculated quality, as if they were chosen to recreate in others the woman's confident perception of herself.

"Rewarding? It's bloody hard work," my mother said. Then she did a strange thing. She moved a step closer to the woman and took hold of her wrist. She placed one of her own hands, calloused and hardened by a half life of digging, pulling, and lifting, next to one of the woman's hands, which were soft and white in the palms and pink around the nails.

"Honey," my mother said, borrowing the affected tone I'd often heard Elsie use on people who needed to have things explained to them. "We didn't go *back* to nature. You left."

The woman was speechless for a moment. She twice opened her mouth to respond, but nothing came out. She took my mother's wrist in her left hand and massaged her palm with the soft fingers of her right hand. She stared at their two hands and said, "You know, you're right. I didn't mean to give offense."

My mother was the kindest person I ever knew. But she was also the most certain about what she believed. And she felt a profound responsibility to set other people's thinking right when confronted with error or contradiction, especially when it came to misconceptions about our family.

"I suppose your way of life has a price," the woman said after an awkward moment. "I guess you have to give up a lot to live the way you do."

"No one has any more to give up than anyone else. Everyone gives up everything in the end. We'll all pay the same price, gratefully. We have no choice."

The woman raised her eyes and blinked as if she were briefly blinded by a bright light.

"What we can choose," my mother said. "Is who gets paid."

The woman's shoulders dropped, her revelatory expression turned blank, and she forced a smile. She took both of my mother's hands in both of her own and shook them wearily.

"Yes. I know."

She released my mother's hands and turned away to rejoin her husband and a young girl, her daughter who was two or three years older than I was, on the other side of the room. She looked back once and my mother nodded, but when she turned away again, my mother shook her head and frowned.

While I watched the woman and her daughter across the room, my mother looked down at me and said, as if the woman could still hear her, "It's not a movement. It's a life."

Chapter 11

Three weeks passed.

Ed and Elsie came to see Jake and Sarah at home. Ed wanted to make arrangements with Jake to begin work. Elsie wanted to convince Sarah to bring June to live on their place while Jake worked. As soon as Ed and Elsie were out of their truck, Jake asked Ed if he'd heard anything about who might own the red cows, and they headed for the corral where the cows were penned. Elsie and Sarah went behind the house to examine the early-autumn remnants of the garden. Elsie took Sarah by the elbow and spoke to her about the man from Olympia. Sarah frowned but did not look at Elsie and did not say anything.

June followed the men to the corral. Ed leaned with his forearms on the top rail of the heavy fence and examined the six Hereford steers. Jake had his back against the fence, while she sat quietly on the bottom rail next to her father with her book resting in one hand on her lap.

"Well," Ed said. "That's nice-looking cattle."

June stood up and turned toward the corral. "They didn't look nearly this good when we found them," she said. "They were thin and a little weak. Herefords don't do that well on the range, and anyway these cows didn't seem like they'd ever been out to pasture much. We've been feeding them hay and letting them graze in the little pasture next to the house."

Ed nodded.

"What should I do with them," Jake said. "They ain't mine."

"Well, you've been feeding 'em like they're yours. I asked around when I was down in Lagrande, and no one seemed to know anything about 'em. Lotta good cattlemen down there, but no one knew anything about any Herefords grazing up this way.

"One old boy did think they might of been rustled. Rustlers in this day and age. Hard to imagine. Anyway, he said about fifty head were stolen off a place down near Ontario early in the spring. Thinks the rustlers coulda dumped the cows off in the backcountry to graze for a few months, and when they went back to round 'em up, didn't bother looking too hard for any strays."

"How do I find out for sure?" Jake asked. "They ain't branded or nothin'."

"I reckon you should just keep 'em for a while anyway. You didn't steal 'em, and they're a damn sight better off in your corral and pasture than they were in the mountains. I'll contact the state police in Oregon, and they can contact the guy that lost the cows. See what he wants to do. But if they ain't his, I reckon you oughta keep 'em. They were on your place, and you've been taking good care of 'em."

"I 'preciate that. But I don't want nothin' to do with another man's cattle. If they was stole, then he should get 'em back."

Behind the house, Sarah was walking up and down the rows of late summer vegetables with Elsie a step or two behind. The day had started out cool, but by midmorning, the sun was shining full force on the garden spot and the air was beginning to warm up.

"I do love this time of the day, this time of the year," Elsie said. "I'm always surprised that you have so much sun here. You're so close to the mountains. If your house was any farther back in the trees, you'd have to plant out here anyway. Too much shade otherwise."

Sarah wasn't really listening. Her thoughts drifted away from her friend back into those same trees. Elsie could see Sarah's mind was elsewhere, but she continued to talk.

"Well, these tomatoes are sure nice. I got some big ones at home, but nothing like these. I use the nitrogen fertilizer Ralph's been pushing on every wife in the county. I swear that man must make a huge profit on that stuff. He says nothing else will work. I got nice tomatoes, but Sarah honey, these of yours…"

She had followed Sarah a few yards away from the garden in the direction of the trees. There was a narrow footpath that curled into the woods and up a small canyon where the creek that watered the garden danced out of the Blue Mountains. Elsie stayed on the path and quickened her pace in order to overtake Sarah, who was walking through the stiff, ankle-high grass.

When they reached the first of the numberless trees, Sarah stopped. Elsie, a half step behind the younger woman, could hear Sarah's labored breathing shallowly rasping in and out. She could see her cadaverous shoulders rise and fall through the flower-thin fabric of her dress. Elsie could tell she was struggling to breathe, even though she held her chin high and her posture remained erect. Elsie took a step forward and reached out with her left hand and placed it gently on Sarah's right arm.

"Honey, are you OK? Should I go get Jake?"

Elsie heard a hoarse cough, and they were close enough to the creek to be aware of the water's noisy progress out of the mountains. Behind the two women were the old house and the garden where green beans on stout poles spun vigorously toward the sky and where blood red tomatoes continued to ripen. Above trees and the mountains, the sun continued its timeless advance toward its apex in the southern sky. Sarah's quiet mind was awash in color—green, red, and green—life, death, and life.

"Sarah, are you OK? Should I get your husband?"

Sarah reached across her body and placed her own left hand on Elsie's. Her breathing had slowed, each breath now less urgent than the one before, and a long, silent moment passed between the two women.

"You know, ever since we came out here to live, there's been one or two days every year when everything is just about perfect. The sun is in just the right place. The wind isn't any more than a breeze. It's not so hot that you're looking for shade all day, but you can leave your coat in the house. The creek's just there, and the mountains are close enough to touch.

"The work's mostly done for the time being. Food's canned and put up. We've got beef on the hoof. Jake'll be making some money and getting hay in pretty soon. Winter's coming and we're ready."

"And June?"

"I'm about as good as I'm ever going to be."

Sarah continued to stand quietly and stare into the forest. Elsie took a step forward and stood next to her.

"You know," Elsie said. "I've lived in this county every day of my life, but I know almost nothing about what's in those mountains. Why, I don't believe I've ever been closer to the mountains than this spot, right here."

"You and Ed use the land. You honor it by what you take from it. And then you give what you take to the world. Wheat. Flour. Bread. Life."

"We make a pretty penny on it too, most years. There's people who think that's not quite right. I don't know."

"Of course it's right. It wouldn't get done otherwise, and people need bread. Wheat and bread take a lot of land. What Jake and I take from the land we mostly keep for ourselves. There isn't much left over."

Elsie took another step forward and stopped a few feet in front of Sarah. She motioned to the woods with her chin. "Did you know that there was a time when much of the land up around our place was covered with trees just like these hills? But my great-great-grandfather and Ed's great-grandfather—my people have been here longer than Ed's. Did you know that? Most people just assume… Well. Those old boys came here a hundred years ago and cut down a lot of the tress, cleared the rock away by hand, and planted wheat. Then a season or two later, they cleared some more land and planted more wheat. Then they bought tractors and cleared more land. More wheat."

"You know what you've got, Elsie. You've known all your life. You knew it when you were a girl. All you have to do is look out your kitchen window to see all that clean land, all that wheat, acres and acres. But I'm afraid to look too closely, as if the truth of my life was hidden away before I was even born. I look out my kitchen window and I see the dark forest. That's my truth. I can see the face of it, feel the truth of it, but it remains dark all around, like that's the way it has to be."

Elsie said nothing. She had never known Sarah to be afraid.

*

When Sarah and Elsie returned to the house, they entered the kitchen through the back door. Jake and Ed were waiting on the narrow porch in front. The sheriff, Tom Bennett, and a tall stranger in a tight-fitting suit were standing in the small space where a lawn might've been. The four men were silent.

Elsie went to the window and moved enough of the ancient curtain out of the way to see what was happening on the porch.

"That's the man from Olympia," she said. "He was at the school board meeting the other night. He said he was going down to Clarkston next. I was afraid he might be back."

As she was speaking, Sarah walked to the door, opened it, and spoke to Jake.

"Ask these gentlemen to come in, please. There's no reason for everyone to stand around outside."

The stranger stepped up onto the porch and walked past Jake and Ed into the tiny living room. The other three men followed, and Jake closed the door.

"Thank you Mrs.—"

"It's Sarah, sir."

"I'm Dr. Roberts. I've come from the State Superintendent of Public Instruction's office."

"Oh my," she said as a small smile crossed her face. "Jake, where's June?"

"I thought it'd be best if she went to her room."

"I'm not sure. But no matter. Let's all go into the kitchen. Where there's more room."

Jake leaned heavily against the counter near the sink. Elsie sat at the table, and Ed remained in the doorway that led from the living room to the kitchen.

"Won't you sit down, Mr. Roberts," Sarah said. She took a seat at the table opposite Elsie, folded her hands, and waited for Roberts to respond, but no one said anything.

He finally broke the silence. "No, thank you. I think I should stand."

June had gone straight to her room. She sat on the edge of her bed with her book unopened in her lap. She knew there were several people in the house but was curious about the lack of any conversation. When she heard Roberts' unfamiliar voice, she left her room and sat quietly on the stairs just below the narrow landing where she could hear everything that was said.

"Your daughter, June is it, has never been to school," Roberts said. "She is twelve years old, is that correct?"

He didn't wait for an answer.

"The problem is that without any professional supervision we cannot be sure she'll ever be in a position to successfully complete the reading, mathematics, and science assessments the state requires. If she does not successfully complete those assessments, she will not graduate from high school."

Roberts paused and took a deep breath. The afternoon had been warm, and his tight-fitting shirt was beginning to rub a sore spot just below his left arm pit. He took a new white handkerchief from his right coat pocket and dabbed at several pearls of sweat that had formed on his forehead.

Just as he opened his mouth to speak again, Sarah said, "I see. Please continue."

Elsie suppressed a smile. Roberts swallowed what he was about to say then coughed once. He composed himself, folded his handkerchief neatly, took another deep breath, and continued.

"Also, your daughter…June…needs to be around other children. Otherwise, normal social development cannot take place."

Sarah unfolded her hands and placed them palm downward on the table. She let her hands slide toward her until she could lightly grip the edge with her thumbs.

"Normal social development?" she said. "Is it normal to expect children to, what, teach each other how to behave or what to think?"

"Obviously not. But a child cannot develop normally living as far removed from other children as June does."

"I see."

Roberts was a tall man. He had once been athletic, but the weight of his knowledge and the strain of his responsibilities had caused his shoulders to droop and his belly to sag so that he slouched forward when he walked, and he had to shift his weight backward onto his heels when he stood still.

"It is the position of the state that your daughter will be in a better place once we get her into school."

"Can you tell me precisely, sir, just how June would be better off there than she is here?"

When she felt crowded, Sarah's voice, language, and demeanor shifted automatically into the same academic formality that had characterized her parents' speech. She understood that the manner in which two people speak to one another reveals much that matters about the participants in the transaction. Sarah's mother always spoke very formally to both her father and to Sarah herself. When her mother did speak spontaneously, it was either the result of mild anger or unpleasant surprise, but she never abandoned formal diction for long. Sarah's father was less formal. Later at school, Sarah herself adopted the habit of formal speech when she discovered careful diction was the quickest way to end a potentially unpleasant conversation with a teacher or other school functionary.

Roberts' measured tone reminded Sarah of her teachers and of principals and school deans when they explained how she must learn to get along and do the same work as the other students. And his imperial manner reminded her of her mother when she explained just how different Sarah was from the other students.

"As I said. The state believes *all* children deserve the best education we can provide. We are afraid that your daughter will get further and further behind if she does not enter school very soon."

Roberts had expressed his *belief* that June may be harmed if she stayed home. June must go to school so she could be protected from a life of ignorance. The law was clear. The matter was settled.

"Further and further behind what? Behind whom?"

"Other students her age and grade level. We're not even sure this child can read."

Elsie spoke up from her place at the table. "I assure you, Dr. Roberts, June reads very well."

"That may be so, but as a member of the school board, you are familiar with state requirements on this matter. There are mandated assessments. We have to be sure. There are tests to determine—"

"June will take no test to determine anything," Sarah said. "I am, we are quite satisfied with her."

"But the law requires—"

"The law does not apply here, sir." Sarah was losing patience. "We have a right to provide for our child without interference."

"This is not interference," Roberts said. "This is help."

Elsie tried again. "Dr. Roberts. The school district considers the child to be home schooled. The state allows for home schooling, yes?"

Now Roberts had lost patience. He stretched himself as erect as he could and said, "You should be aware of the home-school statute, Mrs. Luke."

Then Roberts articulated a widely disseminated bureaucratic untruth.

"There are criteria that must be met. Tests. Assessments. A certified teacher should be involved. That is certainly not happening here."

"But this is how we've always managed home-school children in Pomeroy," Elsie said. "We let them know what the school can do for them and then…we leave them alone."

Roberts pulled back his shoulders and pulled in his gut. "No one is to be left alone. If it can be shown that the child is not flourishing materially or intellectually in the home environment, the law allows us to remove her."

Jake pushed himself away from his perch near the sink. He clenched both fists but relaxed when Sarah glanced in his direction and shook her head. She put both hands on the table and with some effort pushed herself to her feet.

"Looking around here," Roberts went on. "I'm sure you'd at least like to take advantage of the school's breakfast and lunch program. At least June would get two good meals a day. I'm sure that would ease the burden on your finances."

*

Sarah's disdain for school (and all other avenues of authority) was not the result of any specific trauma from her own school days, but rather from the ironic disconnect that grew quite naturally out of the distance between her parents' specialties. The danger of mathematics is that it is sequential and formulaic because its foundation and utility is necessarily arcane. The danger in the academic pursuit of literature is its apparent randomness and abstraction. In the first case the complex is to be made simple, in the second the simple, complex.

As a child Sarah's natural inclinations were to please her parents. She expected at all times to be the smartest kid in the classroom and most of the time to be smarter than whatever adult was nominally in charge. When she was still a child, Sarah simply went along with her parents' expectations. She tolerated the intellectual shortcomings of her teachers and the backwardness of her classmates.

The one constant for Sarah throughout her school years was that her precocious nature was not faked. She really was exceptionally bright. And not just in the sense of doing her schoolwork better and faster than everyone else. The girl demonstrated early that she had an innate perceptive quality that her mathematician mother discounted, but that her scholarly father took great pride in. Like many fathers, though, he was content to defer his daughter's upbringing to his wife. Even so, he was satisfied to see the girl race through the equations her mother gave her each night in order to have more time to sort her way through the extensive library in his study.

One night when she was twelve, Sarah had fallen asleep at the desk in her bedroom. When she woke, she stretched and rubbed her eyes and walked into the hallway. Her parents slept in separate beds in the room directly across the hall from her own room. The door was open, and she could see her parents were both asleep. The house was dark except for the light spilling into the hallway from her room. She had no idea what time it was, but she knew it must be late because her parents rarely went to sleep before midnight. Sarah crept silently to her father's study and snuggled into the large leather chair behind his desk with a book she had pulled randomly from one of the floor-to-ceiling shelves that occupied three sides of the room. *Essays: First Series (1841)* by Ralph Waldo Emerson.

Her father, or one of his students, had marked a particular page with a thin strip of yellow paper torn from a pad. Sarah opened the book and found a passage both underlined in red and heavily marked with a yellow highlighter.

"There comes a time in every man's education when he arrives at the conviction that envy is ignorance; that imitation is suicide."

Sarah read the highlighted quotation several times. She closed the book, holding the place with her finger. She walked to the door of the study and looked down the hallway toward the light from her room. With the book still in her hand and with her finger still marking her place, she went to her room, sat at her own desk, and stared down at the neat equations she had completed earlier.

"Envy is ignorance."

Sarah knew *she* was envied. It was what her parents, especially her mother, intended. She rolled the quotation around in her mind, and for the first time in her life, she was envious.

"…and imitation is suicide."

The quotation settled into an unfamiliar niche at the front of her brain, and, also for the first time in her life, she felt lonely.

She rose from the desk, took a heavy coat from her closet, and left the house with the book still under her arm. The streets of the neighborhood were quiet and sedate even during the day, but in the dank hours after midnight the night air was heavy with Bellingham's familiar dampness. She walked to a lush park nearby and found a familiar dry depression in the side of a low hill among several large evergreen trees where she pulled her legs up inside the over-sized coat and curled into a ball. She hugged the book up under her chin like a literary security blanket and went to sleep.

Sarah's parents were not concerned when she was not in her room the next morning. They often slept late—a privilege unique to senior academics who insist on the right to set their own teaching schedules—and Sarah was often gone to school by the time they woke up. But when the school called both parents at the university to say that Sarah was not there, and when she had not come home long after dark, they became concerned (they never worried). The police were called, and the girl was found quickly sitting beneath a streetlight in the same park staring at the same quotation. When the patrolman who had found her asked what she was doing, she responded by asking him to take her home.

Her mother and father did not run up the walk when she arrived home in a patrol car. The policeman walked her to the door where her parents were standing, her mother in front and her slightly taller father behind and to one side so he could see over his wife's shoulder. Sarah and the policeman stopped at the threshold. The girl did not enter the house.

"Where have you been," her father said. "We've been—"

"You didn't go to school," her mother said. "Your schoolbooks are still in your room."

"She was at the park," the policeman said. "Sitting on a bench reading that book. Said she'd been there since very early this morning."

"Sarah, come in the house," her father said. He took half a step around his wife and took the girl by the hand and pulled her inside. "Let's see what you've been reading."

"Thank you, officer," her mother said. "What do we do next? Are there procedures for incidents like this?"

"I'll file a report, ma'am. We're just glad she's home safe. It's always scary when a child is missing, especially these days. If you folks are OK, I'll just be going."

Her mother watched the policeman until he drove away. Then she closed the door.

Then there was the time Sarah finally gave in. She was still fourteen and an eleventh grader. Her mother was at the university.

Her father was away on some academic retreat. She stared down at the equations her mother gave her to work on and recalled the voice of her English teacher earlier that day.

"Sarah, that is an interesting idea, but it's not what the experts accept regarding what Emerson means to say."

"But the poem does not agree with what he says in his essay on self-reliance. Envy is ignorance."

"The timing and the purpose of the poem and the essay are different. If you can't see that, if you don't understand that, then you've missed the point. Yes, you need to think about what the books tell us, but you also need to know what the various authorities, people who know a lot more about Emerson than you do, have to say. Emerson is not Thoreau. He was much more practically minded. He understood that we need to remain faithful to the values of the community in which we live."

"And imitation is suicide."

"That is not *exactly* what he is saying. Emerson is speaking metaphorically."

Just then from somewhere deep down a private voice whispered into the ear of the girl's soul.

"No!" the girl said. "He meant what he said. You own your own life. *They* do not. I do not believe *any* of you."

"Sarah. Please."

*

Sarah stepped away from the table and took two careful steps in Roberts' direction. She stopped before she reached the man and folded her hands at her waist. Jake had leaned back against the counter near the sink, but his arms were folded tightly, and his fists remained clenched. Elsie also stood up, but did not move from her place at the table.

Roberts glanced from Elsie to Sarah, but he paid no attention to Jake.

Sarah dropped her eyes and said, "Mr. Roberts, you work in Olympia."

"Yes. I work for OSPI, the Office of—"

"I know who you work for. We haven't been here in this house as long as you might have thought. I'm from Bellingham myself. My parents were, that is, both of my parents were professors at the university. I was brought up in a home in which academic achievement of the kind to which you refer was not only valued but was also obligatory.

"We've had quite a number of polite inquiries from school officials in Pomeroy. They know June very well and are satisfied her academic progress is adequate to the life we live here. Since Mr. Dawson, the school superintendent in Pomeroy, is satisfied, why aren't you? What is it you, or the authority you represent, want from us, Mr. Roberts?"

Sarah had never met Roberts before, but she knew him well. He had come to explain things and had not expected any opposition. They were "hill people" after all, uneducated and far removed from the halls of power and the seat of wisdom in the state capitol. He had come with full faith in his ability to convince June's parents that they needed his assistance.

Outside, the sun had begun to set. In the narrow canyons and the broader valleys of the Blue Mountains, darkness had already begun to fall. Much of the county was sliding toward evening, and the few bright corners of the forest were nestling into the warm shadows. Inside the ancient house, sunlight would continue to stream through the narrow windows until just before full darkness fell.

June had moved down the stairs below the narrow landing. She sat on the bottom step, in a bright spot warmed by the day's final sunbeam where she could see the entire kitchen. Her father was still at the counter. Elsie stood at the table, and Ed had moved away from the door to stand next to her. Sarah faced Roberts, her hands folded, and her head bowed. The distance between them seemed to have increased.

"What do you want from us?" she said again. "What do you require?"

Doubt crept across Roberts' face, and a hint of uncertainty concerning his mission began to erode his bureaucratic self-assuredness. He stared blankly at her while he waited for the doubt to diminish. Finally, he made a dismissive gesture with his left hand, a swatting motion in front of his face as if he were batting away an invisible irritant fluttering just beyond the edge of his understanding. He took a final deep breath.

"We want that child in school. I have the authority to insist that this situation is fully assessed. This girl cannot live her life in the woods, cut off from the world and in a state of poverty without suffering long-term social and academic disability. We all want what's best for—"

"I don't believe that to be so. Mr. Roberts."

"It's *Doctor* Roberts."

"*Doctor* Roberts, you have *no* right to my daughter. You believe you have the authority to do with her what you wish. That may be true. Or at least the laws of this state may say it is true, but here… Here you are a long way from Olympia, and your authority is not recognized."

"Mrs. Luke, please, can you help me? This woman needs to understand that we have the child's best interest at heart. No one wants to involve CPS or the sheriff in this. The child *must* go to school."

No one spoke. June moved to the base of the stairs. Finally, the light that had been pouring into the room began to withdraw as the sun disappeared below the nearby hills. Elsie stood and went to the wall near the back door and turned on the single overhead light. Roberts leaned forward to take a step toward Sarah, but when she raised her hand, he stepped back.

"*My* child *must* do nothing."

Roberts sighed. He turned to the sheriff and said, "We should go now. There's nothing more to do here. We're taking this to the next step."

June had moved farther into the room. As Roberts was inching toward the door, she tugged on his sleeve and said, "Sir, I'll be OK. Really. I can read, and I know a lot."

Roberts looked at the girl and frowned. Then he turned toward Sarah and said, "How do we know what this child says is true?"

Sarah hissed through her clenched jaw, "Because she just told you."

Roberts turned to the sheriff and motioned toward June. "This will be your affair soon, Sheriff. I intend to see that the law is enforced." He stepped toward the door, stopped, and waited for the sheriff.

"I'll do what I can, Jake," the sheriff said. "Sarah, I'm afraid he can do what he says. He can take June. At least for a while. Why don't you just go along this time? I'd hate to have to do what he'll make me do."

"Tom, you are as good a man as there is in this county," Sarah said. "If the time comes, you'll do what you have to do. And so will I."

Jake had said nothing, but when Sarah spoke, he stood up and put his hands in his back pockets and said, "Me too, Tom."

"Jake," the sheriff said. "Don't be foolish."

"My husband is not a fool, Tom. You know that."

"The law is the law," Roberts said. "The sheriff will enforce the law."

"The law stops at that gravel road," Sarah said.

"That just ain't so." The sheriff took his hands out of his back pockets and extended his right hand to Jake. "Good luck to you." Then he nodded toward Roberts and headed out the door toward his car.

"Sheriff, wait," Roberts said. "If Ed and Elsie don't mind, I think I'd like to ride back to town with them. I have some things to discuss with the president of the school board."

"My pleasure," Tom said without consulting Ed or Elsie. He left the house quickly, got into his patrol car, and drove faster than necessary back to town.

Outside the house, Roberts confronted Ed and Elsie.

"Will the sheriff do his duty?"

"He'll do what's right, I think," Elsie said. Ed remained silent.

Then Roberts surprised Elsie by climbing into her place in the front passenger seat of Ed's nearly new pickup. She thought Roberts should have offered to ride in the backseat, so she could refuse. Instead, he settled into the front seat, closed the door firmly, and waited for them to get in. Elsie met Ed at the rear of the truck.

"I'm going to invite him to stay the night at our place. Maybe if we get him into the light of day, we can talk him outta making things hard for that child."

"You're going to do what you think best," Ed said. "But I think the man has his mind made up. A man like that won't let go of the notion that a *poor* woman like Sarah got the best of him."

"We'll see. At least I can talk to him."

He left his wife at the back of the truck and got in behind the steering wheel. He waited until he heard her get into the backseat behind him. He started the truck and drove away down the long dirt driveway to the gravel road. The moon was down, so the only light came from the truck's headlights.

Ed stopped the truck when they reached the gravel and waited a long moment while Roberts remarked that the county should provide a light where the narrow dirt track met the road.

"It's not really safe here, is it," Roberts said. "It must be hard to find this place at night."

"I think maybe that's the point," Ed said sharply.

Elsie leaned forward and put a hand on her husband's shoulder and squeezed it softly. "Mr. Roberts, the thing is some of these people just want to be left alone. They do fine. Their kids do fine. Almost all of the folks that live out here have their kids in school and are perfectly happy with it."

"How many families live out this way?"

Ed was afraid she was telling Roberts more than he needed to know. He glanced in the rearview mirror at his wife. She caught his glance and proceeded more cautiously.

"Not that many. Just a few families."

Elsie did not tell him there were only three families living in the mountains near the Oregon border, nor did she mention that no one lived farther from town than Jake and Sarah.

"And how many of these families do not put their students in the public school?"

Ed glanced in the rearview mirror again. Elsie paused, and Roberts spoke again before she could answer.

"The truth is June is the only child in the county not currently enrolled in the Pomeroy schools. From what I've seen tonight that child must be seriously behind her age group in terms of knowing how to behave around adults and we have no way of knowing whether her home-school program has allowed her to reach an appropriate level of achievement."

"Mr. Roberts, that child is way ahead—"

"Elsie, I understand your loyalty to this family, but I'm convinced June is in jeopardy. The state has an obligation and an interest in making sure every child is physically safe and is making appropriate progress. And there is no way to know that in this case."

When Roberts finished, Ed turned right onto the gravel road and headed back toward Pomeroy.

*

June always went to bed when her parents did, but she never went to sleep early. She would lie awake for a long time while the characters of her current book danced across her mind to the music of ideas that endlessly swirled through her mountain home. When June finally fell asleep, she dreamt of the beautiful princess reaching out in the darkness for the god in her bed.

"Why?" the princess said. "Why can't I see you? What are you afraid of?"

"I have nothing to fear, for I am immortal. But you *must* be afraid. You are mortal and must die; you must be perfected, before you can look into the face of God. It's enough that you know I'm here. It's enough."

June awoke with a start. "The face of the god. The face of God."

The rising sun began to shine through the small window above her bed. The first light of the morning settled onto her face while the rest of the room remained in shadow. She opened her eyes and recalled what her mother and the school man had said to each other while she listened from the top of the stairs. She was not certain whether her mother knew she had been listening, but she was certain that what Sarah had said to the man wouldn't have changed whether June had been listening or not.

Chapter 12

My mother was no cynic, but she had come to believe that no one ever says exactly what they mean.

"Everyone recognizes some higher authority. What a man believes depends on to whom he is bound." My mother's grammar often became very formal, as if what she had to say came from a place so deep or so distant that absolute precision was required. I was *only* twelve at the time, still not certain about many things, so I was willing to allow my mother to govern my assumptions and steer my untested faith. But she never insisted that I take what she believed for my own. She did not encourage independence She insisted on it. I think that's why I knew what my mother's response to Roberts would be. My mother was certain. But his faith in himself and in his authority would eventually falter. And he would form another temporary allegiance when it did.

"Very few people really believe what they say," my mother said. "They believe what they are expected to believe in order to get what they need. Money, usually. And other things too. Power.

"June, you will always be able to tell when someone believes what they are telling you because it will not happen often."

Roberts came to our place to explain the law and to demonstrate his faith in the law to my parents, but my mother did not believe a word he had to say because, in truth, Roberts did not believe a word he had to say. From my seat on the stairs, I could hear everything said in our kitchen that night. When I moved down to the bottom step, I could see everything. I suppose my mother knew I was there, but I was very quiet, so I'm not sure anyone else did.

Roberts was at least a foot taller than my mother, a thick man and powerfully built. But, looking back, what he had to say seemed small, as if the legal sinew of his authority was insufficient to support the whole heft of the truth. He had *only* the law to rely on. My mother had her stone cold, rock solid, dyed-in-the-wool, ever lovin', goddamn-it-to-hellfire, convicted self-reliance, an assurance in which my father and myself had absolute confidence.

My father considered the upkeep on our old house a personal challenge. He was engaged in a constant battle with summer's heat and winter's cold. He constantly nailed, caulked, and screened, but the hundred-year-old house, the ageless mountains, and the eternal elements conspired against him. No matter what my father did, the house remained drafty all year.

The temperature dropped rapidly during the long autumn evenings, and even on the warmest winter days, we had to wear long-underwear shirts and heavy sweaters indoors after the sun went down. When Roberts opened the door to leave, he stood for a moment in the doorway looking back into the house toward my mother. A frigid gust eddied around him and into the house from the dark. The chill that remained when he closed the door hung in the house like a callous invader from a dark country. I pulled my heavy shirt tighter and returned to my place at the bottom of the stairs. Ed had moved away from the door to sit at the table while Elsie spoke quietly with my mother. My father continued to lean against the counter with his arms folded and said nothing.

Ed got up and nodded at my father. Elsie stood and held my mother's hand in both of hers. My mother did not rise. In the dim light of the room, she seemed drawn and weak. I noticed that her loose-fitting dress seemed to have grown larger. It sagged sadly off her skeletal shoulders, and I believe her hand trembled. Elsie said something to Ed then turned to look at me. When they left with Roberts, I went to the table and sat across from my mother and placed my book in front of me. My father left his place by the sink to stand behind me with both hands on the back of the chair. The chill dissolved and I felt safe.

"Do you understand what Dr. Roberts wants us to do?" my mother said.

I opened my book and put both hands, palms down, on the pages. "Yes. He wants me to go to school, and he says he can have the sheriff take me away if I won't go."

"Yes. That's right."

Outside the darkness had settled completely. The old house groaned as the temperature continued to drop. Inside, in a dim circle of yellow light at the kitchen table, my family remained silent. My father took his hand from the back of the chair and massaged my shoulders with his fingers. I remember especially how the elegant lightness of his touch conveyed a sense of limitless strength as I stroked the pages of the book with my own fingertips. My mother's hands were folded, and she tapped her lips with the knuckles of her bent thumbs.

Finally, she looked up and said, "Jake?"

"No," my father said. "We can't, and they won't."

*

My father did not waste words. Once a matter had settled in his mind, he did not consider the issue further, and he always meant what he said.

Of the things my mother believed—no—of all the things she was certain about, the most fervent was that love and coercion, adoration and constraint, cannot coexist. The truth cannot be imposed by any authority. Since her love for me was unconditional, unfathomable, and ultimately, unspeakable, she would not surrender my life to any arbitrary authority. If love is the language of God, then coercion, accommodation, and compromise are the language of the devil. She knew we each must discover the truth anew and on our own terms.

She knew almost everything about the plants and animals on our place because she watched, waited, and listened. She never bothered with books about nature, farming, or gardening. She watched and noticed. She made adjustments. If something did not work, she found out why and changed the way she did it the next time. One time, a year or so before Roberts came to our place, I came into the house with a large, round tomato. I held it in two hands, not because it was too large to carry in one hand, but because the tomato was so nearly perfect in form and firmness. It was a profound joy to feel it against my fingertips and in my palms.

"Look at this one," I said. "It's perfect. Mom, this one is too good to eat."

"No, June." She took the tomato from me and hefted it up and down a time or two and held it close to her face. "It's pretty close, though, isn't it? Maybe next year or the year after. In the meantime, this one will go very nicely with our beef steak tonight."

My mother's reaction was not false modesty or extravagant humility. "There may be no such thing as a perfect tomato," she said. "But we'll never know if we grow them exactly the same way every year.

"You will never know the truth. But if you pay attention, you can move in that direction. You can get closer and closer and closer until finally you'll stare reality in the face." I am now certain that reality was finally revealed to my mother, and even now she is eternally contemplating the face of God.

The revelation that defined my mother's early life was the realization that her own parents, especially her mother, had brought her into the world, not to give her the opportunity to gaze someday into the face of the truth, but to glorify their own lives, to elevate their own vision for their own sake. My mother's parents had created her to complete an equation: One plus one equals all there is, when one is all there is.

Chapter 13

The next morning arrived late. The autumn chill took longer to dissipate because the dark remnants of a storm from the west had rolled up against the Blue Mountains, suggesting the possibility of rain later in the day. June woke to the confused lowing of the red cows, still restless in their new surroundings. She took her book downstairs and settled into her usual spot at the kitchen table to re-read the story of the princess and her invisible lover. She looked out her window and thought about how impenetrably dark the princess's bed chamber must have been.

"There must've been no windows," she said aloud. She loved to lie in bed on the rare night when the glow of the moon through the window in her room produced just enough light to read by. "The princess wouldn't need a candle if the moonlight could shine through a window?"

Her mother and father came downstairs later than usual, and June stopped reading and listened as her parents talked about how soon Jake would need to go to Ed and Elsie's to begin work on the harvest machinery. Roberts' visit was not mentioned.

"I gotta start thinking about getting on up to Ed's place," Jake said. "You and June should come with me. We need the work, and I'll feel better if you two are close by."

"I'll think about it," Sarah said. "June, honey, what would you like to do?"

June closed her book, knowing she could return to the same page without having to search. "Well, the cattle here will pretty much take care of themselves if we let them out into the south-end pastures. I don't know what would happen to the red cows if we turn them back out, and I'd be worried about the horses, but there's plenty of grass in the front pasture, and the creek's got all the water they'll need."

"Yes. But what would you *like* to do?"

"Well, I guess that all depends on what needs to be done."

Jake smiled, and Sarah nodded her head, proud. June's entire world was contained by the life of the ranch. She was not distracted by typical childish frivolity because everything that happened in her world had immediate and discernible consequences. Even her play, to this point, had a joyous utilitarianism about it. June played on purpose.

"I'll do something about those red cows before I go to Ed's," Jake said.

"I guess you two can go on up to Ed and Elsie's," Sarah said. "Maybe I'll just stay here and look after things."

"I can't leave you here, the way you been." He glanced quickly at June, who did not react. "No. We all gotta go to Ed's."

"How *have* I been?" Sarah also glanced quickly at June, who was stroking the pages of her book with her fingertips and watching her parents. "And how will going to Ed and Elsie's change how I'm going to be?"

She stared at him, not in anger, or even irritation, but in contemplation of what had just been said and what might come next. After a moment he turned away and left the house through the back door. She nodded her head slowly then walked across the kitchen and placed a hand on June's shoulder. She squeezed slightly but said nothing.

"Mom, is the princess ever *allowed* to see him?"

"She's just like us. And the god is a god. Perfect in the way of the story. The princess is…human. She couldn't stand to see the god's face, not in her present state. That's in the story too. She has to change, but she has to *be* changed first."

"So, the god is protecting her?"

"I suppose. From herself maybe, from her human imperfection."

Sarah paused. June opened her book. She turned a page and read the first sentence. Something brushed against the back of the house outside and she and her mother both looked up and turned in the direction of the noise. Jake was repairing floorboards on the back porch. There was a scraping sound then the rasp of a handsaw. June returned to her book and read the second sentence. For just a moment, Sarah continued to stare off in the direction where her husband was working then she turned back toward her daughter.

"June, my mother and father were good people. Accomplished people. You owe your good mind to them. But when I was your age, I noticed there was a flaw. They believed in perfection, human perfection. Their intention was for me to be perfect, so I wished to be perfect.

"To my mother, my life and hers too, was like an equation. You just had to keep calculating, adding what was certain and subtracting foolishness until the sides balanced. Then…perfection."

Sarah stopped again to collect her thoughts and catch her breath. The rhythmic banging of Jake's hammer had replaced the rasping of the saw. She loved to listen to Jake work. She imagined the care he was taking to make sure each floorboard fit together seamlessly. She knew he would be working slowly, choosing each rough cut 2x6 carefully, measuring twice, double-checking so the dark pencil line he drew to guide his saw was perfectly square. He would pull the saw backward against the edge of the board three times to create a notch deep enough to guide the first few strokes of the saw. Before he put each floorboard in its place, he'd brush any loose splinters off the cut end with his fingertips and check to make sure there were no obstructions to prevent the boards from fitting together snuggly. He would tap the half inch-long tongue on each new board into the half inch-deep groove of the floorboard already nailed down, making sure the joint closed seamlessly along its entire length. Then he'd tap the board back toward the house until the ends were flush. Finally, he'd nail each end of the new floorboard to the 2x6 joists. Sarah imagined her husband standing back a step or two after each board was nailed into place. He'd inspect his work, nod his head, and whisper "perfect" then move onto the next section of the floor.

"Life might be an equation, June, but I'm not sure we have the solution. All we can do is keep our balance. There's a time for everything. Every…thing. But we often aren't allowed to know what it is."

"The time was not right for the princess," June said. "But she thought it was. The princess doesn't want to wait, does she? She doesn't understand. Then her sisters come, and…"

Outside, the wind preceding the storm picked up. Sarah felt cold, so she walked to the other side of the room and laid a small fire in the big wood stove. June was silent, knowing her mother would think about her question before she answered, and she needed to do something while she thought. Sarah took a large wooden match from a box on the windowsill above the sink and struck it against the side of the stove. The match sparked, and a modest flame began to grow out of the chemical glob at the end. She turned it upside down and watched as the flame grew and crawled slowly up the wooden matchstick toward her fingers. She turned the match upright again and touched the flame to the shredded kindling Jake had whittled from an old cedar fence post. The tender flared and she threw the remnants of the match into the grate and closed the door. When she was sure the kindling would ignite, she returned to the kitchen table and sat down across from her daughter. June waited. Sarah folded her hands and pursed her lips.

"Her sisters come from the world the princess has left." Sarah always spoke of books in the present tense. "Do you see? When she chooses life with the god, she agrees to one rule. She may not see his face. Her sisters have no claim here. Do you see what happens when she does what her sisters want instead of what she's promised to do? She loses all she has and all she is."

June glanced down at the words. She thought about what her mother had said. When she looked up, Sarah had her eyes closed. Her head was down, and her breathing was slow and very deep. In and out, then a pause. Then in and out again. She watched her mother. She thought about how Sarah had looked the night before when she confronted Roberts. Her dress seemed to have grown too large. It hung from her shoulders and was wrapped around her like a shroud. The girl felt a dull thrill in the pit of her stomach. She thought the dull thrill must be fear, but she was not certain because she had never been afraid.

"Mom, are you going to die?"

June's questions often caught Sarah off guard, so she was always careful before answering. This time she felt something click in her chest, and for the first time in many years, she thought she might lose control of her determined certainty. She took two deep, panicky breaths and put her hand on her heart. She felt the irregular beat and began to curse the unnamed disease that would soon steal so much. She thought about her daughter and about her future. She thought of the princess and the final candlelit glimpse of the god. And finally, she thought about all that would be lost if she did not cling faithfully to the truth, if she did not fend off the fatal desire to live beyond her time. She squeezed her hands into brittle fists to get control of her breathing.

She looked up and gazed into her daughter's eyes for a long time and said, "Yes, June, I am going to die."

*

A pall had settled on the canyons and narrow valleys south of the house. The storm left behind a measure of sadness and the forest was quiet. The rain did not fall, but the threat of it had driven the life of the forest into the shelter of the dense evergreen canopy on the hillsides and narrow crevices between the rocks higher up. The storm suggested danger, but shelter never fails.

Jake finished the repairs, then stood on the covered porch and watched the clouds roll up against the hills. He returned to the house and went upstairs. June was still at the kitchen table when her father returned. He gripped his Winchester, and pointed the barrel pointed toward the floor. He wore a webbed military-style gun belt with a .45 caliber pistol in a leather holster on his right hip.

"I'm going to take a ride. Your mother's in the kitchen. She knows where I'm headed."

"Why are you taking your guns?"

"Don't make sense to have anything on the place that you don't know how to use. I'm goin' to ride off down toward the south end and shoot off a few rounds. Target practice."

"Want me to come with you?" June had no fear of guns. Her father had taught her to shoot, and she knew how to clean and load all of the weapons he kept in the house, just as she knew how to handle most of the other hand tools on the ranch. Yet she had never seen her mother with a gun.

"No. I'll go on by myself. I think your mother might need some help with the garden in a bit."

Jake followed the creek and disappeared into the woods riding toward the south end of the ranch. Sarah came outside carrying a large yellow bowl of green beans and stood next to June on the newly repaired back porch. She sat on a stiff-backed wooden chair and snapped green beans from the bowl in her lap. June sat on the new floorboards with her back to her mother and her feet resting on the dirt. Sarah smiled when she remembered how June's feet used to dangle above the ground.

"You're getting taller every day."

The girl did not answer.

Sarah wasn't sure she had responded correctly when June asked about dying. The girl had inherited both her mother's thoughtful nature and her father's reticence. June spoke openly only when she was sure she knew precisely what she wanted to say. She would not develop the inevitable adolescent tendency for spontaneous self-expression. Sarah did not expect an emotional response from her daughter, but she had expected questions. When the girl finally spoke, Sarah was surprised by what she wanted to know.

"Mom, why does Mr. Roberts even care if I go to school or not?"

"It's the law. The law says that every child must go to school. Are you sure you want to talk about this now?"

"Yes. Other kids go. Why shouldn't I?"

Sarah thought of her own mother. She rubbed her forehead with the fingertips of her left hand.

"Mr. Roberts didn't seem like a bad man," June said. "He seems like he wants to do the right thing."

"He does. I'm sure he does. But what's the right thing?"

"Elsie would say to follow the law."

"So would Mr. Roberts, and Elsie knows you better than anyone. Elsie wants what is best for you, and she thinks you should be in school."

Sarah stopped talking and June waited. The sharp report of Jake's rifle caused both to look away to the south. The flutter in her chest brought Sarah's attention back to her daughter. Her dress had sagged off her left shoulder. She set the basket on the ground and shrugged the dress back up and straightened it with her hands. The clouds continued to roll up against the mountains, and a chill breeze drifted down through the small canyon from the woods. A stronger wind bent the treetops away from the house, and the air became heavy and damp. A second rifle shot echoed up from south of the house.

"What does Mr. Roberts want?"

"Do you remember the story of Jesus and the learned men? They were the keepers of the law. They believed you had to obey every word of the law to be saved. They said God *demanded* obedience, 'even unto death.' Well, Jesus told them they were not the law. He told them they were using the law to glorify themselves. He told them He'd come to complete the law, to make it clear enough for anyone to understand."

"The law is simple then?"

"The law of learned men is not simple."

"But you said the law of Jesus is simple."

"And so is the law for your princess. 'Do not attempt to see me in the light.' It doesn't make sense in the practical way we like to see things, but it is, for her, the law. And it is what it is.

"I think Mr. Roberts believes the law is right, but that doesn't mean that what's right is the law. I don't believe he wants you in school because of the law. He wants you in school because *he* says so."

"Do you not want me to go to school because *you* say so?"

Sarah didn't want to answer. She didn't want to face the possibility that her attitude about June going to school was the result of her own sin. Was it certitude and resolution, or was it pride and defiance? The gentle wind that had drifted down from the mountains earlier raced back up the canyon away from the house, and the leaves in the small orchard to the west fluttered noisily as the breeze departed. Sarah shivered and felt the certitude that had been so settled at her core begin to freeze.

"Maybe. I hope not. Maybe Mr. Roberts and I want the same thing."

The breeze stopped for a moment, and a third rifle shot filled the gap.

June stood and turned to face her mother. "When you said you were going to die this morning, I felt afraid. I'm still afraid."

Sarah stood and reached out to take her child's hand. She pulled June to her and put her arms around the girl. June stepped forward and nuzzled in close. The wind rose again and rattled the windows of the old house and then dissipated. The clouds slid over the highest ridges south of the ranch and rolled on east toward Idaho. Behind the storm, a bright sun in a cloudless sky, and the vague doubt began to soften and melt away.

"I know you're afraid. But I'll be OK. Remember the better place. Don't forget, we'll all be there together."

June took one long, deep, shuddering breath. She climbed onto Sarah's lap and put both her arms around her mother's neck. She did not let go and she did not cry.

Chapter 14

I wonder.

Does fear come from some unknown place deep within us, or do we learn fear from those around us? Did fear draw me toward my mother or did it push her away? The princess had been warned, but she still shined a flickering light on her divine lover.

I remember.

After my father rode off to the south end of our place to shoot his rifle, I did something I hadn't done since I was a very small child. I crawled into my mother's lap. I suffered no lack of affection from either of my parents, but I also don't remember too many times when that affection was demonstrated physically. My parents, especially my father and at particular times my mother, would often, as an expression of approval or concern, lay hands on me. I remember my father's rough hands when he patted my thigh after he showed me how to use a tool or pulled my heel down to make sure my stirrups were the proper length. When I completed a new task just the way he had explained it to me, he would place his hand between my shoulder blades and nod once to indicate satisfaction and once again to indicate approval. My mother would occasionally put her hand on my forearm and lower her voice to focus my attention during a lesson or pat the back of my hand when I grew impatient or frustrated. She would sometimes massage the back of my neck when she was unsure of what to say.

In the mountains where we lived the passing of each season, and the birth and death of each new day was clearly delineated by the natural rhythms of the earth and the sky.

Sunrise. Sunset. Swiftly flow...

I have since learned that most people live their entire lives in the absence of darkness. In the city the shadows cast by streetlights and neon signs create pockets of near dark into which most people never go. Other farms and ranches had powerful yard lights that cast a yellow circle, creating a cosmic fence that kept predators and scavengers away from houses and barns. Invisible coyotes would rustle the wheat stubble at the verge of the yellow circle, but, despite eternal hunger, they would not cross the stark margin into the unnatural light.

With no yard light, and with lights inside the house finally turned off, a deep and primal darkness would settle onto our place on moonless nights. I never left the house at night, but I would often stand on the back porch well before sunrise and stare into the void. I don't know if my eyes adjusted to the blackness or whether I could discern a slight movement in the nearby trees because I already knew what was there. And the night often seemed tainted by a faint canine pungency. Sometimes I would try to penetrate the darkness with my father's powerful flashlight. I would slowly sweep the light back and forth but could never see anything other than a narrow and incomplete image of the world beyond the safety of the porch, and occasionally the quick withdrawal of a gray or brown tail low to the ground.

I was never afraid of the dark. In fact, it was the indistinct glare of the flashlight that made me uneasy. I felt quiet and secure when I turned the light off. I could see nothing. But I knew what was out there, and I had faith that my solid apprehension of the world would return in a sun-drenched revelation in the morning. I'd sit in my mother's chair on the porch and wait for the new light to slowly reveal, in ever-deepening detail, the warm fact of my familiar world.

Then my mother told me she was going to die, and a mortal darkness settled onto my life. I asked her for the light of reassurance.

I had grown as tall as my mother, and she had become frail, but I settled into her lap, and she put her thin arms around me. I could still smell the sawdust from the new floorboards on the back porch, and we both looked up at the sharp report of a rifle far away to the south.

I put my head on her shoulder and whispered into her ear. "When?"

"Soon, I think. The time seems about right."

Light at last.

Chapter 15

When Jake returned to the house, June had not moved from her mother's lap. He reigned in his horse just before he emerged from the trees at a spot where he could see his wife and child on the newly repaired back porch. He had not seen June cuddled in her mother's lap for some time, but the sight did not surprise or alarm him. He waited until she got down and went in the house and then nudged his horse forward. Usually, he would've ridden to a hitching post outside the corral and unsaddled his horse, but this time he rode around the garden and stopped near the sturdy steps of the back porch.

Sarah's head was down, and her chest was rising and falling slowly as if she were asleep. Jake did not move and did not speak. Still grasping the reins, he placed his hands on the saddle horn and settled back against the pommel. The horse dropped his head and settled back on his hind legs and relaxed, and Jake waited for his wife.

When Sarah looked up, her eyes were still closed, and her hands were folded in her lap. She inhaled deeply one more time and then opened her eyes. The first thing she saw was her husband sitting on his horse. She smiled at the sight.

"Jake, I don't think I've ever seen anyone who looks so right sitting on a horse. It might be that you and I don't belong in the present time."

"And this place?"

"A time and a place aren't the same thing. I won't be leaving this place."

"What about me and June?"

"She knows."

And for the first time, *certainly* for the first time, so did he.

The sun had climbed above the trees and the day was getting warm. A silence surrounded the house along with the last oppressive heat of the fading summer. Jake's horse swished his tail and snorted.

"That horse knows you're done with him. He wants to go to the barn corral and eat. You'd better unsaddle him and put him away."

"Sarah, what am I gonna…Where are we…"

She stood and stepped to the edge of the porch. She reached out and touched the horse's face and stroked the kind spot between his eyes. The horse leaned forward so she could reach him more easily. Jake took off his hat and set it on the saddle horn. He ran his fingers through his hair and turned his head away for a moment.

"Jake." Her voice was steady, certain, and calm. "You'll know what to do."

"There's not much time, then?"

She walked carefully to the steps. She put one foot down gingerly onto the first step and paused. Jake shifted his weight in the saddle and reached out with his right hand. She looked up at her husband and then took the last two steps to the ground without looking down. She reached up and took his hand, and he pulled her toward him. He leaned over in the saddle and kissed his wife on the top of the head.

When he sat up again, she looked at him and said, "There's always more time than we need."

Chapter 16

My mother had time.

My father and I did not.

It would be common to say the events of the next several days were a blur. But they were not. I remember every detail, every distinct moment.

First.

My mother died sitting in the sun on our new back porch with a bowl of beans on her lap. I found her late one morning several days after Roberts had come to our place. She seemed to be asleep, but I knew she had died. Our porch was situated so that the sun would shine on it most of the day, so her skin remained warm for a long time.

My father gently laid her body out on the porch and then wrapped it in a blanket that had been folded at the foot of their bed. We lifted her across the back of one of the saddle horses and walked her body along the creek into the shadow of the woods to the spring where I had once seen her bathe naked and where my father had already dug an ample grave. He liked to complete necessary tasks well before they needed to be done.

"If you wait until you need something," he told me on more than one occasion. "You're likely to rush and not do as good a job as you might."

I don't know when he dug the grave, but I gave no thought to the fact he had. It was only some years later when I thought about those days that I realized my mother must have spoken to him about what she wanted done. I wonder still if she was with him when he dug the grave. She must've selected the spot, and she would've given him very specific instructions about what was to happen when she died because my father did not hesitate. He never hesitated once he knew what to do.

Still, his hands shook when he lowered her into the ground. He told me she had insisted that there be no coffin. He took a long time to fill in the hole, and he left no mound. I helped him level the ground. We used evergreen boughs to brush away all evidence of our presence there, and the next substantial rain would erase any trace of the grave. My father and I would know where she was buried, but no one else would. Ever.

He led the horse back down the trail along the creek, but I stayed behind. I did not cry, exactly, but there were tears. They flowed in long warm rivulets down my cheeks and dripped from my chin. I dropped to my knees and scooped a handful of dirt from my mother's invisible grave and held it next to my heart for a long time.

What I did next seems strange to me even now. I don't know what compelled me. I was only twelve and my adolescent body had only recently begun to take on the womanish form my mother had been losing. The beginnings of the fecund roundness seemed to me to be both the anatomical vestige of who my mother had been and the animate token of the woman I would become.

I replaced the dirt and smoothed over the tiny depression. I stood and walked to the edge of the small spring. It flowed shallow, warm, and quiet that late summer. I removed my boots and my socks and placed them neatly far enough from the water so there was no chance they would get wet. I pulled my thin dress over my head and placed it folded on my boots. I slipped my hands inside the elastic waistband of my cotton underpants and pushed them very slowly down to my ankles and placed them on top of the dress with my toe.

I stood naked and uncertain between my mother's deep grave and the shallow mountain spring. I wiped the last tear from my cheek and stepped into the cold water. In the middle of the spring, I dropped to my knees just as my mother had done and was surprised by the soft grittiness of the sandy bottom. On my knees, the water reached my bare shoulders.

I stood and waded gingerly out of the spring. I then stood shivering next to my mother's grave. I did not pray. Not for relief. And not for understanding. My mother was there in the dark, and I did not have a candle. I gathered up my clothes, put everything except my boots and socks back on, and with a boot in each hand, I was nearly skipping as I followed my father's path down the trail and back home.

Second.

Roberts returned.

The day we buried my mother, he came to our place with Sheriff Tom and a woman from Clarkston. My father stood on our small elevated front porch. I watched from the open front door as Roberts, the sheriff, and the unknown woman approached the house. Roberts put his foot on the first step and began to step up.

"That'll be far enough," my father told him. The woman had moved up close behind Roberts, but the sheriff had taken a step back. "What is it you want? We've told you once. You have no business here. I'd take it kindly if you'd leave."

Roberts took another step toward the porch and my father moved to block his way. I moved out of the doorway onto the porch, behind my father and a little to the left.

"Sheriff," Roberts said. "Would you explain the law to this man, please?"

Tom moved up next to the steps, but he stayed on the ground so he had to look up at my father. "Jake, where's Sarah?"

"She's not here."

I could see the sheriff lower his eyes and rub his lower lip with the thumb and forefinger of his left hand, but Roberts could not.

"Where's the girl's mother," Roberts said. "It would be best if both parents were present for this."

"I told you she's not here," my father said, and there was an edge to his voice that caused me to catch my breath and hold it.

"Jake, we need to talk to the both of you," the sheriff said. "We need to talk about June."

My father reached back and took me gently by the arm and pulled me in close. Then he let go of my arm and put both hands in his back pockets.

"Then talk."

"I don't think she should be present while we discuss her future," Roberts said, meaning me.

There are moments that we never lose. Small things. A glance. A touch. The turn of a phrase. A tone of voice. Little instants that in total and in retrospect account for more of what we know about the people we love than all the grand gestures put together. My mother delighting in the perfection of a carrot as she held it up to the light. My father's satisfied nod after he'd nailed a floorboard perfectly into place.

My father stared at Roberts. His chin trembled and his hands were shaking. He removed his hands from his back pockets and clenched his fists, and I leaned in closer to him.

"June is here, and she'll hear what you have to say."

"What about the girl's mother?" the woman behind Roberts said. It was the first time she had spoken.

"She's not here," I said to the woman. "I am."

Chapter 17

The woman was Roberta Crump. She was younger than Roberts, though not by a lot. She worked for the State Child Protective Services. It was her job to make sure that the children in southeastern Washington were well fed, well cared for, well educated, and safe. She and her agency had extraordinary power to make extra-legal decisions about whether the home environment of a child was appropriately nurturing. In fact, school employees were required by state law to inform local police or CPS authorities whenever they even suspected a child might be in danger. School employees were held legally accountable if they failed to do so, as if they'd abused or neglected a child themselves.

No one in Pomeroy had reason to suspect June was in danger, so no one thought to notify Ms. Crump or her agency. Roberts, though, was certain June's education was being neglected, and he suspected her well-being was in jeopardy, so he made a call to CPS in Walla Walla, and Ms. Crump was sent to evaluate June's living situation. Of course, Roberts insisted on going along.

"Tom, what's this about?" Jake said from the porch.

Roberts had stepped back onto the ground next to Crump. Jake walked slowly down the steps and June moved to the edge of the porch.

"Why are you here with these people? What do they want?"

"We are here—" Roberts said.

"I'm talking to Tom." Jake could feel a long-buried rage begin to rise in his fists and forearms, so he jammed his hands back into his back pockets.

"Jake, this is an official visit. Ms. Crump here has the legal right to look around to see whether —"

"To see whether the home environment is appropriate for the upbringing of a child," Crump said.

Jake stood up straight and pulled his head back. "Safe? 'Propriate? Tom, what's going on here?"

June had been watching her father, but now her eyes moved past Roberts to Crump. She could feel a residual dampness in her arm pits, and her dress was lightly smudged with brown dirt from her mother's grave. Her hands were still dirty. She had become aware, for the first time, of an adult tightness pushing at the worn fabric of her dress at her breasts and in her hips.

"I'm not a child." She didn't shout, but Jake heard in her tone and intention, the certain voice of her mother. "I can take care of myself. We don't need you."

Crump ignored June. "Where's the girl's mother, please? Are there any more children or is June the only one?"

Crump moved toward the steps, but Jake blocked her way.

"Excuse me, sir," Crump said. "I have the legal right to enter this house and to inspect all adjacent premises. If you do not allow me to do so, the sheriff will detain you."

Crump's certainty surprised Jake. She seemed just as determined to interfere with the life of his family as Sarah had been to preserve their independence. Crump's certainty scared him in the same way Sarah's had consoled him. He opened his mouth, but did not speak.

June did.

"No, he will not. This is our home. You've no right to be here."

Jake turned to look at her, but Roberts and Crump continued to ignore her. The sheriff had retreated to lean on the fender of his patrol car parked next to Jake's truck on the hard ground a few feet in front of the porch. He had removed his hat and was brushing his close-cropped hair with his left hand.

Roberts took a bold step in Jake's direction. Jake reached out and put his right hand in the middle of the school man's chest. Roberts stopped, but Jake did not take his hand away.

"Sheriff," Roberts said. He looked back over his shoulder toward Tom Bennett. The sheriff had stood up and put his hat back on. He took two tentative steps toward the house.

"Jake, these folks are right about the law. You got to let Ms. Crump have her look around, and then you got to go along with what she decides to do about June."

"It would help if the child's mother were present," Crump said.

"My mother's not here, so you might as well leave. There's nothing here for you to see."

"Tom, do we have to do what these people say?"

"Jake? Sarah. Is she…Did she?"

"She's not here, Mr. Bennett," June said. She turned away quickly and went inside the house.

The sheriff dropped his eyes, stared at the ground, and spoke in a reverent whisper. "I see."

Jake removed his hand from Roberts' chest but did not back away.

"Well, I don't see," Crump said. "Sheriff, I intend to see what's going on in this home, and you will make it possible for me to do so."

"I'm not sure this is the right time for a visit," the sheriff said. "Let's head on back to town and come back another time."

"This is the perfect time," Crump said. "I'm here and I will do my duty. Sheriff, please do yours."

Crump stepped around Jake and onto the porch. Roberts began to do the same, but Jake put his hand up again and pushed Roberts hard in the chest. Even though he was much larger than Jake, the force of the push caused Roberts to stumble backward.

"Jake, don't," the sheriff said.

Roberts quickly regained his balance and started for the porch. Jake put both hands out this time and when he pushed Roberts, the school man's feet slipped out from under him, and he sat down awkwardly.

On the porch, Crump shouted at Tom Bennett. "Sheriff! Arrest him for assault!"

The sheriff moved in Jake's direction but was stopped by the sound of a gunshot. Crump screamed and then froze. Roberts scrambled backwards toward the sheriff's car. Jake did not move.

Back on the porch, June had fired a shot from her mother's .32 caliber pistol into the floorboards. She then raised the gun toward Crump and held it with her right hand resting on her left as her father had taught her. She held the weapon steady despite its weight. When the woman from CPS saw the gun was pointed at the center of her chest, she began to shake.

"Oh…God. That child has a gun. There's a gun in the home." Then she began to recognize her situation. "Don't shoot. Please, don't shoot."

"I told you I could take care of myself," June said. "We don't need you here. I'm not leaving. This is our home. You have no right to be here."

"Sheriff," Crump was pleading.

"June, honey, put the gun down," Tom Bennett moved toward the porch. "Give me the gun, sweetheart."

"I will put the gun away when these people leave. Please take them away, Mr. Bennett."

"We're leaving right now," Roberts said. He had crouched behind sheriff's car and was peeking out from behind the trunk. "Ms. Crump, let's go, now."

June still held the gun on Crump, and the woman did not move.

"June, give me the gun," Jake said. He stepped slowly onto the porch and placed himself between Crump and the girl.

She lowered the gun, released the hammer, and placed it in her father's hand. He removed the magazine, ejected the chambered cartridge, and tossed the gun to the sheriff. Crump, released from the terror of immediate danger, stepped down from the porch without taking her eyes off June. She stumbled backward a step then turned and ran to join Roberts behind the sheriff's car. The sheriff tapped the gun absentmindedly against his right thigh. Jake sat on the edge of the porch and looked up at Tom.

"This ain't good, is it?"

Bennett approached him so he could speak without Roberts and Crump hearing. "They're not going to let this go. As soon as those two get themselves under control, they'll convince each other that I got to arrest someone. I know June wasn't going to shoot that woman, but the threat is enough."

She had moved to the steps and sat down. Roberts and Crump had stood up, but they remained behind the sheriff's car out of earshot.

"If that woman'd tried to go in the house, I think June might've shot her," Jake said. "Sarah ain't here."

Bennett didn't ask where Sarah was. He knew. But he also knew if he forced Jake to tell him, he'd have to do something about it.

There was nothing to do that he thought would be helpful, so he didn't ask.

"I ain't going to arrest you. But I'm going to have to explain to those two why not. They won't be satisfied with anything I say. They'll call the State Patrol and report that you knocked Roberts down and that June threatened Crump with a gun and that a shot was fired.

"The state cops will call me to see what happened, and I got to tell them what I saw. I'll explain the situation, and that might cause them to think a while before they come out here, but everyone knows you got guns here, so the state police will be pretty cautious when they show up."

"How long do we got?"

"They'll be here tomorrow morning. I'll tell them you're no danger to them, but they'll still come expecting trouble."

"I can't let them take June away, Tom. You know that."

"Yes, I do. But you knocked a representative of the State Department of Education on his butt, and your daughter threatened a Child Protective Services official with a gun. That don't add up to an easy time for you and June."

"Maybe we should leave for a while. Let things kinda settle some."

"I can't tell you what to do. I'm still the sheriff, and I got a job to do here. I think I know what you got in mind, but don't say anything to me about it."

The sheriff put his right hand on Jake's shoulder. "I wish that Roberts fella had listened to Elsie in the first place. I wish they'd just left you folks alone. I'm sorry about Sarah. She was—she's a fine woman."

Bennett turned away and headed toward his car. "June, honey," he said as he walked away. "You take care of your daddy, ya hear. And be careful with the guns."

"Yes sir, Sheriff. I will."

Bennett opened the back driver's side door of his car and motioned for Crump to get in. Roberts got in the front seat. Bennett turned once more in the direction of the house.

"Jake," he said with a small wave.

"Sheriff." He nodded in return.

The sheriff got into his car and drove back to Pomeroy.

June looked up at her father. She stood, walked over next to him, and took his right hand in her left. Together they watched the dust cloud settle as it followed the sheriff's car down the long driveway. Jake put his arm around June and held her close. He tried to place his chin on the top of her head, but she was too tall.

"My lord, girl, you're taller than your momma. I reckon we got to leave for a while. God, I'm tired, though."

She rose up on her tiptoes and kissed her father on the cheek. She went back into the house. Her book sat open on the kitchen table. She closed it then went to the sink and began to wash and peel the same potatoes her mother had dug from the garden that morning.

Chapter 18

My father's greatest gift may have been foresight. But can grief be mitigated by good planning? My mother would've said *yes*.

I thought about foresight in the damp hours after midnight as we rode slowly and silently to the top of the ridge and down the other side. When my father rode, he sat erect, straight as a post and perfectly balanced. But we broke out of the trees at the top of the ridge, and our way was briefly lit by the full moon shining through a break in the clouds. I could see his shoulders hunched forward, and he seemed to be trembling. Then the clouds covered the moon, and he became a vague shadow again.

I think he has remained so in my mind ever since.

When we reached level ground at the bottom of the hill, he stopped, and I rode up next to him. He was sitting up tall and straight again.

I have not yet grieved for my mother, even after all these years. I think the time has not come...yet. I thought of the book in my saddlebag and wondered if the darkness that separates us had anything to do with something I was not permitted to know.

Until the time when… Will the time ever be…right?

I was surprised when my father loaded the saddled horses into our trailer after the sheriff left. We could've ridden easily and on familiar ground straight south from our place into Oregon along the same trail we'd taken when we brought the red cows up. But no. My father had the gift of foresight, and he had something else in mind.

It did not occur to me then, but now it seems remarkable that we never wanted for anything, even on the day my mother died. There were years when weather or cattle prices conspired to reduce our income to almost nothing. But neither of my parents ever spoke of money, at least not in my presence, but I don't ever remember doing without anything that mattered. Somehow there was always enough to eat, wood for the fire, and warm clothes that fit. Roberts and Crump assumed we were poor and needed their help. But people like that only know of want. What could Roberts and Crump possibly know of need?

We left the sheriff sitting in his car. My father was not convinced Tom would call the state police immediately. There was a special sort of understanding that existed between Tom and the people who lived in Pomeroy and Garfield County. My father once remarked that he didn't come down to our end of the county unless there was a serious problem or unless some higher civil authority insisted.

Serious problem? Higher authority? Any difficulty my family faced was mitigated by a higher authority in which Roberts and Crump had no faith because the force came from a place outside their own desire. See…I can speak like my mother when I get serious.

"Tom don't much care what folks in the mountains do," my father said. "As long as what they're doin' don't hurt no one else." The closer a family lived to town, the more interested the sheriff was likely to be. If you lived *in* town, he paid close attention, interested in everything.

I wonder what my mother would have said about Tom and a higher authority. What would she have considered a need serious enough to set aside what she knew and trusted? I think she would've said something about the difference between what Roberts and Crump meant by authority and what Tom understood about the limits of his authority.

Crump and Roberts invaded our home in the name of an authority that served nothing but their own position. Tom came along to make sure *his* people were not abused by that authority.

"It's just politics," Tom told my father before he drove away with Crump and Roberts that day, and I wondered if he meant the same thing Elsie meant when she said, "It's only school." Or did he mean it the way my mother did when she told Roberts, "The law does not mean anything here."

I wonder.

I've had almost six years to think about all this. The state has given me ample time and little space and nothing much else to concern myself with. Once a week I talk to my father on the phone. Each time we speak, my enclosure seems to have whittled a deeper notch into his spirit.

We never speak of my mother, but she always seems present. From that first night riding in the mountains, when the dark seemed impenetrable, almost solid as we let our horses feel their way over the ridge and down the hill. To this day, I have from time to time been aware of my mother. I've heard her voice clearly, much more than a shadowy memory taking shape in an opaque forest. When I mention the voice, my father tells me he often dreams of my mother. But a dream is not the same as a voice in the dark. My father and I are both saved by the durability of my mother's passion.

Elsie comes to visit once a month, even though it's a long drive from Garfield County. She always brings a book. She tells me Ed sends a couple of men down to our place a few times a year to make sure the old house is in good repair. They check on the gates and even fix the fences when it's necessary. She promises I'll be able to live there, maybe even with my father, when all this is over, and she always says "I'm so sorry" when she leaves.

I think she feels guilty. She shouldn't. I did what I did, and guilt is as pointless as grief.

Now I stare into the dark outside my cell. I hold a candle up and am careful not to let the hot wax drip. Sometimes I think I get a glimpse. Then there is the rustle of a thin kitchen dress on a still night and the vague image of my mother recedes. Like the impatient princess in the myth, I'm still not permitted to see her face.

Chapter 19

Tom Bennett sat in the county's green-and-white, four-wheel-drive pickup and tapped his fingers on the steering wheel. He knew precisely what he should do. He should radio the state police and report that he'd found Jake's truck abandoned in the mountains and that Jake, and probably June, had ridden together over the ridge into the valley on the other side. Jake knew the mountains well, so Tom understood the location of his truck would be very important to the state police.

"Nope," he said aloud. "I ain't goin' to do it."

He got out of his vehicle and climbed into Jake's truck. He knew most people in Garfield County were careless with their car keys, and he was pretty sure Jake never took his truck keys out of the ignition. He was right.

He started the truck and carefully drove away from the barrow pit and headed about a mile down the dirt road toward where he knew there was another, even narrower road that veered off to the east and ran between two steep hillsides. The road had not been used for a while and was partially overgrown in spots so the truck and trailer trailed broken bits of tree branches as Tom maneuvered carefully through the dark.

When Tom reached a slightly wider spot in the road, he steered the truck up against the hillside and pulled forward so the right front bumper and fender scraped away a bit of dirt and rock. He made sure the trailer was as far off the road as possible. Then he put Jake's keys in the pocket of his fur-lined denim jacket with the Sheriff Department insignia sewn over his left breast pocket. He got out of the truck and began to amble back to where he'd left his truck.

It took Tom forty-five minutes to walk back to his own rig. He was winded, but he felt good. *Got to get more exercise,* he thought as he climbed into the county's heavy, four-wheel drive SUV. Tom always drove the SUV when his official duties took him into the mountains. He took off his Stetson and flipped it onto the passenger seat. He ran his fingers through his hair and wiped sweat from his brow with the sleeve of his jacket. He took the microphone from the dash and flipped on the radio.

"Base, this is Tom. Are you there?"

"It's Hobart, Sheriff. You find 'em?"

Tom paused for a long moment before he answered.

"Nope," he said. "No sign of 'em at all. They must of drove on down into Oregon. I'm heading back to town."

"Roger that, Sheriff."

*

Jake did not feel entirely safe until he and Jill had reached the top of the ridge and started down the other side. He listened hard for any audible sign that Tom Bennett was following, even though he knew

Tom was a prudent man and unlikely to come after them on foot, especially in the dark. But Jake still paid attention.

There'd been a fire on the ridge some years before, so the hillside had been thinned. Jake noticed the faint black smell of soggy ashes and burnt wood and could feel saplings brush gently against his legs as the horses maneuvered among the trees that had survived the fire. He hoped he and June would not find the valley floor scorched.

When they reached the top of the ridge, and he was certain they were safe, he was overcome by the sudden awareness of what had been lost when Sarah died. He slumped forward in the saddle and began to shake. He transferred the reins to his left hand and grabbed the saddle horn with his right to steady himself. His panic passed quickly when he heard a voice from somewhere to his left.

"We're going to be OK." He thought it was June who was speaking, but the voice he heard had the clear hard certainty of his wife. "Just trust your horse, remember?"

He sat up tall again. He turned back to June without stopping his horse and said, "I remember. Let's keep moving." She waved at her father and kept moving down the hill.

The dark descent was much steeper than the hill on the other side of the ridge, which rose slowly away from the dirt road where Tom Bennett had stopped to check their truck and trailer. Jake slowed his horse and told June to stay close. Dense clouds covered the moon creating a nearly impenetrable darkness.

Jake could barely see the ground in front of his horse. The horses weaved their way slowly downward among the generously spaced trees, which appeared to be dark holes in the damp blackness rather than living things. He continued to listen, but the weight of the damp air seemed to hold back all sound except the rhythmic creaking of saddle leather and the soft, careful padding of the horses' hooves. The heavy silence and the faint, close-by smell of damp ashes stayed with him until they reached the valley floor.

Soon the hard rain returned, and water dripping off his sodden hat made seeing the ground even more difficult. He was worried that June might be getting cold, but the girl and her little mare continued to follow his gelding without complaint. The horses were careful, and he could feel his mount begin to take smaller steps and shift his weight toward his back end as they worked their way down a steeper stretch. He had no idea about how far they had to ride before they reached the valley floor. He had no knowledge of a trail, so his only certainty was to keep going down and to let his horse find the way. He looked back frequently to make sure June was following closely. He knew the girl had to be getting tired and he wanted to get to the valley floor and find a suitable place to camp before it was fully daylight.

As they neared the floor, the rain stopped. He would make a quick survey of their surroundings when the full moon would occasionally appear through a break in the clouds. The trees were closer together now and dark green in the moonlight rather than black. There was no sign of forest fire here, and he wondered if he'd imagined the small of ashes. He was heartened when a soft, green pungency replaced the ashen mustiness of the rain as they rode out of the trees near the valley floor. The hillside began to flatten out, and the sky above the ridgeline lightened a bit. They came out of the trees into a broad meadow. He stopped and dismounted.

"Let's give the horses a break," he said.

When June rode up next to his horse, he took her reins while she dismounted. He noticed her stumble when she stepped down. The girl had never learned to complain, so when she said, "I'm really tired, Dad," he knew he needed to find a place to set up a cold camp, and soon.

"We'll rest here for a few minutes," he said. "We need a bit of daylight to make sure this meadow's not too swampy to cross. Then we'll hunt up a place to sleep. We need to be hard to find for a couple 'a days."

She sat down with her back against a tree. The ground was wet, but she was dressed warmly, and her heavy slicker kept her bottom dry. She leaned back, and he thought she might've gone to sleep. With the reins for both horses in one hand, he crossed his arms and rested his head against June's saddle. He closed his eyes and felt the panic of loss begin to rise again.

"No," he said out loud. *I'm going to hold it together.* When her old aunt died, Sarah told Jake and June that grief was natural, but useless in the end. "We'll be sad for a little while," she said. "But we don't have time to carry on too much or for too long."

Is this a better place, Sarah? He crossed his arms on the horse's rump and stared across the meadow and watched the darkness dissipate. He closed his eyes and might've slept briefly. *Is this what you wanted for June?*

Then he heard the voice again, as from a shallow dream. It seemed to be coming from somewhere down the narrow valley. Jake turned toward the voice and saw a vague light between two trees. *Find a place to sleep. Tom's not going to be any more helpful than he has to be to anyone from outside. It'll be Roberts and Crump that will get the state police involved. Besides, you'll be in Oregon soon. That will make it harder. You only need a little more time.*

The voice stopped, but the vague light remained, fading away as daylight advanced. The sun had not yet appeared above the ridgeline, but the dark was nearly gone. With the reins for both horses still in his right hand, Jake bent forward and gently touched June on the shoulder.

"We got to find a better place to camp. Right, Dad?"

"Yep. We best get goin'. I'll bet there's some good shelter on the other side of this valley."

She stood up and he started to help her mount.

"No," she said. "I'm OK." She reached up for the saddle horn but had to hop several times on her right foot to get enough momentum to pull herself into the saddle.

"But let's not go across the valley," she said. "Remember where our cattle always bunch up in bad weather? If there's any dry shelter, we're more likely to find it up that way."

He nodded. "I 'spect you're right."

They followed the verge of the meadow toward the narrow end of the valley. He was surprised to see a narrow trail in the grass. He stopped his horse and dismounted. He took a step or two up the trail, then stopped and dropped to one knee to examine the ground.

"Someone's been this way," he said. He stood and turned toward the hillside they'd just descended and stared hard into the trees. There was just enough underbrush to conceal anyone who did not want to be seen.

"What is it?"

"Footprint. Got to be recent too, or the rain would of washed it away. Someone's been on this trail goin' the same way we are and not too long ago."

She sat up straight and gazed across the meadow while Jake searched the hillside.

"I don't see anyone," she said.

"Me neither."

"Maybe we'd better go back down the valley."

He was silent. He continued to scan the hillside. Finally, he dropped to one knee again and looked at the footprint. He returned to his horse and stared across the animal's back at his daughter. He thought about Sarah.

"I don't know, June. What do you think your mother would say to do?"

Her throat tightened, and her eyes felt hot and scratchy, but she did not cry. She listened for a voice in the wilderness.

Silence.

He continued to look up at her, waiting.

Finally, she said, "Out here…She'd leave it up to you. She'd say you'd know the right thing to do. Trust your horse, Dad."

"I got a feeling about that footprint," he said. He remounted and settled into the saddle. "We'll go on up the valley. Why don't you go first, and I'll follow along and keep an eye on things back here. Follow the trail. They usually lead somewhere."

She yawned. "Or away from somewhere."

"Well, girl…away's where we're trying to get."

She squeezed the mare gently, and her horse moved slowly up the trail. Jake waited a few seconds because he wanted some distance between the two horses. He sat up straighter and continued to scan the near hillside. He saw no sign that anyone was there.

But, about a quarter of a mile ahead, a man on foot had climbed about fifty yards off the trial. He moved silently and just fast enough to stay far enough ahead that June and Jake would not be aware he was watching.

And he knew where the trail ended.

*

Rupert Grim was a lost soul, by choice.

Rupert continued to watch Jake for the twenty minutes it took to reach his permanent camp at the end of the valley. He lived in the mountains for as much of the year as the weather would allow. When it turned colder than he liked, he hid his tent and summer gear in a shallow cave. He'd hike to a trailhead where he had an old truck locked up, drive down to Lagrande, and catch a bus south.

June reined in her horse and looked back to Jake coming up the trail about fifty yards behind her.

"Dad, you better come up here and look at this."

He kicked his horse into a careful jog and then reined in as he drew up next to her. What they saw was a substantial canvas tent tucked into a flat spot under a rock overhang. The tent was the most dominant feature of a neat semipermanent campsite with a wooden picnic table and a stone-fire pit. The tent flaps were tied shut to keep the interior dry, but a shallow puddle of rainwater had accumulated in the seat on a nylon camp chair placed in front of the tent. Just as Jake was about to pull the rifle from the leather scabbard under his right leg, Rupert appeared in a crouch on the ledge just above the tent.

"You won't need that rifle, sir," Rupert said and then stood up. They were startled, but Jake kept his hand on the rifle, which he'd pulled halfway out of the scabbard. "I'd relax, if I were you, and put that gun away. I mean you no harm. I think I've got a pretty good idea why you're up here."

"You been followin' us," he said. "I thought I heard someone speakin' in the woods back there."

"I didn't say a word," Rupert said. "But I've been watching since you left Tom Bennett sitting in his truck on the other side of the ridge. I'm glad you didn't shoot. I'm told you generally hit what you aim at."

"Told? You've been following us all night?"

"I didn't want you to make a wrong turn and…well, it's not real safe riding around these mountains in the dark."

"The sheriff…"

"Tom Bennett is a good man," Rupert said. "That's probably why he let you go."

"How would you know about us?"

"Well, let's see. The sheriff is after you, so you must've done something someone thought was bad enough to involve the law. That doesn't mean whatever you've done is actually wrong, so to speak."

Rupert turned away from them and disappeared. In a few seconds, he reappeared from behind the tent and took hold of June's reins. Her chin had dropped, and she slumped forward struggling to stay awake. Rupert reached up and put his left hand on the girl's shoulder.

"Come on down here, young lady."

"Don't," Jake said. He started to pull the rifle out again.

Rupert held up his right hand then supported June with both hands as she slid out of the saddle. Jake put the rifle away.

"I think we should get this child inside the tent. Then you can tell me as much as you'd like about why you're out here. Take your girl. The tent is dry, and there's a clean cot. I'll get her bedroll."

Jake dismounted, walked around the back of the horses, and swept June up into his arms.

"This way." He led Jake into the tent. It was darker inside, but it was tall enough for Jake to stand upright in the center. Rupert folded his own sleeping bag and removed it from the only cot in the tent. He unrolled June's blankets and arranged them on the cot so Jake could fold the blankets over her after he laid her down. Then he stepped back, waited for a moment, and left the tent. Jake carefully removed June's riding boots and set them on the ground beneath the cot. He folded the blankets over her and put his hand on her forehead and thought of Sarah. He left the tent and found Rupert sitting at the picnic table.

"I never thought we'd run into anyone up here. I don't know who you are, mister, but I'm grateful. We left home so quick, and I never thought how hard this might be on the girl. Her name is June."

"I know her name. And it's a lovely name. But I guess we should talk about why you're up here with such precious cargo. Then I'll see what I should do about it."

Chapter 20

Rupert Grimm saved us.

My memories of that morning are incomplete. It's been a long time, and I had fallen asleep on my horse. I didn't know how I got onto the cot in Rupert's tent, but I knew where I was when I woke up. Rupert's cot was a welcome luxury. My father would have made an adequate camp, but I expected to sleep on the ground, probably under a tree. Still, I didn't sleep in the tent for very long, and when I woke up, my father was gone. He'd led the horses to a steam that ran off the steep hillside at the narrow end of the canyon and down through the meadow. I knew he would stake the horses out so they could graze and drink from the stream while he watched them.

When I woke up and found myself alone with a man I'd never met, I wasn't afraid because I hadn't yet learned to fear strangers and because my father wouldn't have left me with Rupert Grimm if there had been any danger. Besides, the animals had to be fed and watered, no matter what our circumstances might've been.

I sat up on the cot still wrapped warmly in my familiar bedroll and looked around. I found my boots at the foot of the cot where I knew my father would leave them, pulled them on, and laced them all the way up. I stood up and listened for a moment to the midmorning sounds of the mountains. I could hear water running somewhere nearby, some sort of bird whistled, and there was a scratching noise that seemed to be coming from outside at the back of the tent. Inside against the far wall was a large plastic box with a lid, but I couldn't imagine what must be stored in it. Two canvas bags that appeared to be filled with clothes were piled on top of the box.

A bookcase at the back of the tent was filled with more books than I thought could be carried to such a place. Pots and pans all about the same size, which had been scoured clean since their last use, were stacked neatly on a low-folding table near the door. The tent was neat, orderly, and spotlessly clean. Even the nylon floor had been swept recently. Next to the bookcase was another set of shelves where dozens of cans and boxes of food were stored. I realized I was hungry and could smell wood smoke. I went outside and realized my father and the horses were gone. Our saddles were propped up on the ground with the saddle pads and our headstalls and bridles draped neatly over the back end.

I don't know why I'm recalling all these details, but they seem to matter. Something about the order and arrangement of Rupert's camp has stayed with me all this time.

Rupert Grimm was sitting on the far side of the wooden picnic table reading my book. Behind him a pot suspended from a thick remnant of a tree branch steamed over a deep bed of coals in the fire pit. He closed the book and stood up when I came out. He was a strange-looking man, taller than my father and obviously much older. He reminded me of pictures I'd seen of men from an earlier century, men who traveled great distances with only a faint hope of finding a small piece of fertile ground at the end of the trail. There was also something disconcerting, something familiar in the way he leaned over the book and in the way his eyes scanned the page.

He was hatless, and now that I think about it, I don't think I ever saw him with a hat. He had long hair, gray near the temples, and had not shaved for a long time. He wore heavy denim pants, a green flannel shirt, a heavy waist-length, flannel-lined canvas coat, and the kind of thick-soled boots I'd seen people from the city wear when they stopped in Pomeroy for lunch or fuel. His clothes were wrinkled and soiled from living in the mountains, but they were of good quality and without wear. His bearing was erect. His eyes were tired, although I don't think from exertion.

Yes. This is how a man from an earlier century who had survived the hardship of the overland journey might've looked, rough and able. But Rupert Grimm spoke clearly and carefully, like a man with something important to say who does not want to be misunderstood.

"Is this your book?" He stood and reached out toward me with the book in his hand. I approached the table but did not take it. "Your father took this from your saddlebag and left it here. I hope you don't mind that I've had a look at it."

"No, sir, I don't mind, but I also don't know who you are."

"Rupert Grimm, formerly Dr. Grimm, but now just a curious wanderer." He paused and looked at me, then offered the book to me again. This time I took it from him.

"As are you too, I see. At least for now."

"Do you live here?"

Rupert made a sweeping gesture with his hands indicating the entire camp. "This place is more of a weigh station. I have a need to be alone for much of the year, but I've no desire to freeze. I'll head south before the snow comes and return in late spring, perhaps early summer."

"You're not a doctor anymore? I've never been to a doctor."

"Oh…I was never a doctor the way you mean. I was never a *healer*, although I may've been a *soother* of souls once, but no more."

"I don't understand. You said you were a doctor."

"A doctor of letters. An expert in the healing power of books. I dispensed biblio-therapy in measured doses of relief gleaned from pages and words. A doctor of…philosophy and theology." He bowed his head and bent at the waist. Surprisingly, I had an urge to giggle but managed to suppress the impulse.

"Love of knowledge and the science of God," I said.

"Well…yes. How would a schoolgirl like yourself know such things?"

"I've never been to school."

"I see. Such things are not generally taught in school anyway, at least not to those of your tender years. Here, child, sit at my table. I'll get you something to eat, and you can tell me about your book and how you are able to so easily explicate Greek and Latin."

I sat down on the bench on the near side of the table. Rupert brought me oatmeal in a wooden bowl and then sat down across the table from me.

"I think most young girls would be afraid to find themselves alone with someone like me," he said. "Your father has gone to—"

"Feed and water the horses. And, since he left me here with you, it must be OK. I'm not afraid of strangers."

"No?"

"No."

"Hmm."

Rupert got up and walked a small circle around the fire then sat down again. I didn't move.

"I've had a little talk with your father. I'm very sorry about your mother."

I remember a catch in my throat and a burning and scratching sensation behind my eyes. I looked away and held the book tightly to my chest then turned back to Rupert. I think his eyes were damp.

"My mother has gone to a better place."

He blinked and then slid his hand across the table, but when he couldn't reach me, he paused and withdrew it. He lowered his eyes, whispered a few words, and touched his chest. "I know of such a place. Perhaps more than I should."

It was at that moment that I began to realize that Rupert Grimm and my mother were somehow connected, and now I know the connection. Both had raised a candle and stolen a glimpse of the Face of God. I opened my book to "Cupid and Psyche" and pushed it across the table toward Rupert.

"Do you know this story?"

"Child, I know all the stories."

Chapter 21

Beloved by its residents, Bellingham, Washington is, in every way, as far removed from the Blue Mountains as any city in Washington State. Bellingham is far enough north to have its own identity distinct from the Northwest's regional capital in Seattle. Although by the time Rupert began to doubt his labors at Western Washington State College, Bellingham's identity was often in crisis and its diverse tribes of conflicting world views were often in conflict. Loggers and academics. Tree huggers and real estate developers. Union mill workers and the bosses. Local residents and shoppers from Canada.

The old town sits on Bellingham Bay, a rocky, southerly facing horseshoe, the last watery refuge in a vast and often turbulent inland arm of the Pacific Ocean. To the north is Prince Rupert Sound, a stormy passage that separates Vancouver Island from the rest of Canada. To the southwest is the Strait of Juan De Fuca, which was once mistaken by a Spanish explorer for the long-sought Northwest Passage. A quirk of Ice Age geology and of nineteenth-century diplomacy is responsible for the fact that Bellingham is actually some fifty miles northwest of British Columbia's provincial capital city of Victoria in Canada.

There are times when Bellingham's weather seems to come from everywhere at once. In late fall and early spring, storms from the frigid Gulf of Alaska pick up speed through Prince Rupert Sound and hammer Bellingham from the north. Sodden North Pacific weather systems gather moisture passing through the Strait of Juan de Fuca. Occasionally violent weather from both directions converges on the city at the same time. Since it's less than twenty miles to the foothills of the Cascade Mountains and only twenty more to the glacial slopes of Mount Baker, the weather has nowhere to go. So, Bellingham in March and April is damp, dank, and dreary.

Then, with the coming of the sun in May and June, the winter and spring moisture that settled in the loamy soil in the surrounding hillsides sets off a green explosion. There is a greater variety of dense vegetation in Bellingham and the surrounding countryside than almost anywhere else in Washington.

*

On the last day of April, Rupert sat at his desk at Western Washington State College and contemplated his last moments as *Dr. Grimm*. He'd already decided he would not teach his last class of the day, so Rupert did not contemplate very long.

"I'm done," he said out loud. "Done."

His settled life began to change when his daughter finally left, and his wife turned on him. Near the end of the eleventh grade, the girl started to skip classes at Bellingham High. And then she'd disappear for days at a time during the summer months. She refused to return to school for her final year, even though she was not yet sixteen. She'd leave the house every morning as if she was going to school and then return home in the late afternoon, just as if she'd been to school.

Neither of her parents questioned her about this, although officials at the school had called several times to report her lack of attendance. The girl's mother and father spoke about the situation only once.

"She must've found a boyfriend," her mother said. "It's the only explanation."

"She's never shown much interest in boys," Rupert said.

"What else could it be?"

"Ask her."

"She'll come up with a clever lie."

"She's never lied before."

"Not that we know of."

"I don't believe she'd lie."

And so it went on for another month. Finally, one day as he left the university, he told the secretary in the English Department he'd not be in for a couple of days. The next morning Rupert waited in his study until he heard his daughter leave the house. He watched out the window of his room as the girl headed up the street carrying a heavily laden backpack.

A cold rain accompanied by a stiff northeasterly wind had soaked the street and the nearby park during the night. The wind and rain continued so Rupert pulled on a heavy sweater, a bland tan raincoat and wool cap with earflaps. He rushed downstairs and out of the house and followed his daughter up the street at a discreet distance.

After several blocks, she turned into the park and trudged on a dirt and gravel pathway through the sodden trees until she came out the other side. When she reached the sidewalk on the far side of the park, she turned left. Rupert rushed toward the sidewalk so he wouldn't lose her, but stayed back among the trees so he could see where she was headed. The girl was waiting at the corner for the light to change. She shrugged her shoulders and wrapped her arms around herself to ward off the rain and wind. Across the street was the brick and stone edifice of Saint James Episcopal Church. The light changed, and the girl crossed the street, stepped quickly up the broad stairs, and entered the church. Rupert stepped out of the trees and onto the sidewalk to follow.

He hurried across the street against the light and waited at the bottom of the stairs. A city bus passing on the street behind him came too close to the curb and splashed frigid water onto the bottom half of his legs. He jumped forward when the water hit him, and his momentum caused him to place one foot on the bottom step. He hesitated for a moment, and then jogged up the stairs and through the same door his daughter had gone through.

The narrow foyer was much warmer than Rupert had expected. The dry heat emanated from a noisy boiler somewhere in the bowels of the building and seemed to be enhanced by the darkly stained wood, dim lighting, and stone floor. The girl was nowhere to be seen. A stairway to Rupert's left went down into what must've been the church basement and another stairway on the right went up into what he assumed must be extra seating above the sanctuary or maybe the choir loft. He tried to remember the last time he'd been inside a church.

He looked up, and over the door was a stained-glass window that would have illuminated an image of the *Madonna and Child* had the sky outside not been the color of slate. The floor-to-ceiling doors of the sanctuary were propped open and immediately opposite the stained-glass window a life-size crucifix dangled from the wall above the altar. The shadows of the darkened sanctuary obscured the face of the crucified Christ.

Rupert stepped to the doors of the sanctuary but did not enter. He turned to look at the image in the window again. The sky had lightened, and as the image brightened, he became aware of the musty smell of old books.

Then he heard a loud snapping noise. He turned around quickly, just in time to see a bright floodlight illuminate the face of the man hanging from the crucifix. His gray eyes seemed alive, and Rupert could not look away from the man's face.

"Did you know you're dripping on our floor?" A smiling man in a dark coat was treading lightly up the center aisle of the sanctuary, but Rupert did not look away from the face on the cross. There was another loud snap, and the image on the cross went dark again.

He shook his head and looked down to where the water from his soaked pants and raincoat was dripping onto the stone floor. "Oh…I'm sorry. I'm looking for a girl."

"A guy in a raincoat looking for a girl…" the smiling man said. "I'm not sure we can help you."

"No, no. I mean I'm looking for my daughter. I saw her come in here a few minutes ago."

"I'm Father John. If you're looking for Sarah, you've come to the right place."

Father John guided Rupert out of the doorway and onto a bench on one side of the foyer. He told him Sarah was in the church library. "She came in here to get out of the rain one day. At least that's the excuse she gave. She had a bag full of books, so I asked if she'd like to see our library. It's quite extensive."

"She's been in your library, all day, all this time?"

"Well, she's usually here in the morning. I think she goes to the college library in the afternoon."

"But our house is full of books. Maybe she's read them all, or—"

"Or she didn't find what she was looking for."

Rupert was silent for a long time, then he frowned and said, "I'm not sure we ever thought much about what she needed."

"Sarah and I've talked," Father John said. "I've tried to draw her out, to get her to tell me something about her life and her family. It's a natural impulse for someone with an evangelical bent. You know, to find an avenue of desperation to draw the unsaved into the church."

"She's never been, that is, we've never been to church."

"I've never seen her here on Sunday. She didn't want to talk about herself or her family. She only wanted to talk about books. Theology. Philosophy. History. I never did find that avenue of desperation. I'm not sure there is one. She may have her own, built-in evangelical impulse."

Neither of Sarah's parents was prone to self-doubt. But Rupert did wonder from time to time, especially as he watched Sarah and her mother race through complicated equations, whether self-certainty was just another form of delusion.

"I'm an English professor. I've given her books to read, but we've never talked about them."

"You might have a hard time keeping up," Father John said. "I do. She's quite brilliant."

Rupert stood up to leave.

"Do you want me to take you to her?"

Rupert shook his head. "I am grateful to you, Father." And he left the church.

Three months later, Sarah left home as usual and did not return. No one heard from her for more than two years when she sent a letter to her father telling him she planned to marry. Two more years passed, and she sent another letter telling Rupert he had become a grandfather and that she planned to settle in a farmhouse in the mountains near Pomeroy, a town he had never heard of. The grandchild's name was June. *I just thought you should know where I am,* the letter said. Sarah's mother was not mentioned.

"My daughter was brilliant," her mother said when it had become apparent Sarah was not coming back. "Now she's quit school and run away. What am I supposed to tell our friends?"

"We don't have friends," Rupert said. "We have *colleagues.*"

"Doesn't matter what you call them. They'll see that we've failed. Well, I didn't fail. She could do the math. It's the goddamned books that turned her against me. Your goddamned books."

"Not my books. Not mine."

On the day after Sarah disappeared, Rupert took her place in Father John's library. Five more years in the church library passed before he decided to follow his daughter.

*

The spring term had just begun, and he had just finished a lecture on *The Grapes of Wrath.* He covered all the conventional subtopics. The Great Depression. The New Deal. Progressive politics. Steinbeck's experience living with migrant workers. A political novel that changed the course of the twentieth century. He articulated all the correct positions on all the right issues.

Then he asked his students, "Has anyone actually read this? Seen the movie? Pondered the title?" The only movement in the room was an awkward nod when a sleeping student's chin slid off the heel of his hand. Then a half-dozen tentative hands went up.

Jesus. What's the point?

"I have a question, Dr. Grimm." The speaker was a stocky, dark-haired young woman with an earnest ponytail.

"Yes, Gloria. What is it?"

"Well, it seems to me that the book reinforces a lot of the traditional male-female roles. Did the writer believe that women should only…"

"No. In fact Ma Joad…"

"Because Rose of Sharon is completely helpless. She'd die if it weren't for…"

"No. Not at all. She is the salvation of the dying man in the final…"

Another student spoke up, a bit older than the rest, clean shaven and wearing a red tie. "That scene is disgusting. It's pornography."

"Remember what Stein—" Rupert said.

"It's still disgusting."

"And it's her mother that makes her do it," Gloria said.

Rupert pulled a chair away from the wall and sat down. The class waited. The boy who had been asleep rubbed his eyes.

"Ma Joad doesn't say a thing to Rose of Sharon. She just looks at the girl." The young man in the tie shook his head. The boy who had been asleep giggled. Gloria stood and started to speak, and Rupert made a halt motion with his hands.

"We're done here."

Gloria sat down. Rupert stood up and left the room.

In his office, he turned his desk chair around so he could see the view through his window. The school rested precariously on the steep slope of Sehome Hill above Bellingham Bay. Rupert gazed past the smokestacks of the paper mill at the bottom of the hill toward the gray water of the bay and the San Juan Islands, barely visible in the hazy distance.

His window was halfway open. The singular chemical aroma of wood chips being cooked into pulp coalesced with the fishy stench of the waterfront and drifted through the window. He wondered why the air in Bellingham so rarely resembled the clean saltiness he'd found remarkable in other Puget Sound cities.

It must be the mill. Progress stinks.

He still had his dog-eared copy of *The Grapes of Wrath* in his hands. He stared at the cover, a crude drawing of a care-worn migrant family staring at the promise of a lush California valley spread out below them and generations of hardship at their back.

There's more here than politics. The Promised Land. Jim Casy wanders alone for forty days. Tom Joad is blinded crossing the creek. You don't know what you're a doin'. Twelve Joads. Grampa isn't allowed to cross over. Jonah. Thomas. Rose of Sharon. The baby floating away down the flooded creek. The milk of human kindness and Salvation at the end.

"I'm a fraud," he said to the open window. "A book is never just one thing."

So, he rolled a sheet of paper into his typewriter and typed two words. *I'm done.* He signed his name and placed the note in an envelope.

"Good-bye, Phyllis," he said to the department chairman's secretary after he handed her the envelope. "I'm leaving."

"Rupert," she said. "Wait. What do I…"

He waved once as he turned away and strode down the hall. He didn't want to wait for the elevator, so he took the stairs down four flights and exited the building through a side door.

It had been a gray day, typical of Bellingham in early spring. But the clouds were breaking up and Rupert noticed the smell from the mill and the waterfront was less pungent on the ground than it had been in his office. He walked east out the back of the campus to a long footpath that climbed for half a mile through a pristine arboretum to the top of Sehome Hill. At the summit was a hundred-foot tower with an observation deck that resembled an old-style fire lookout.

He climbed to the top of the tower and surveyed the city. He gazed out over the vast, gray suggestion of the Pacific Ocean to the west then turned toward the certainty of the Cascade foothills and Mount Baker to the east. He leaned on a railing and looked down, but he could not see the paper mill, just smoke and steam belching into the sky. The smoke leaned to the north, blown away along with the sour odor by a middling breeze. Rupert inhaled deeply through his nose and was pleased to smell saltwater.

He climbed down and made his way by another trail off the hill and into the streets surrounding the campus and walked three miles home. On the way he stopped at the bank and emptied all his accounts. He and his mathematics professor wife had always kept their finances, like everything else, separate. The only thing of substance they had shared was Sarah. *But she's gone. Some little town on the other side of the mountains.*

His wife's classes ended before his, so she was sitting in a deep armchair waiting for him when he came through the door.

"Phyllis called," his wife said. "She said you threatened to quit."

"I didn't threaten. I'm done. I'm sorry."

"Me too."

"You're done or you're sorry."

"Yes."

He did not speak. After waiting a short time for a further response from his wife, which didn't come, he went upstairs to his small study and took two books from his shelves. *Essays: First Series (1841)* by Ralph Waldo Emerson and *Greek Myths and Legends*, which had been compiled and edited by a colleague at the university. The man had signed his name on the title page. Halfway down the stairs, he stopped. He turned and bounded back up the stairs and into the room his daughter had once occupied. In a desk drawer, where it had hidden undisturbed for all these years, he found a Bible. Inside, on the page for listing family members and ancestors, he found only two names, his own and Sarah's.

Ten minutes later he was on Interstate 5 heading south. He would turn east at Seattle. He had no idea how long it would take to drive the nearly four hundred miles to Pomeroy, but he was determined not to stop except for fuel until he got there.

*

When Jake returned to the camp with the horses, June was scraping the last bits of oatmeal from the bottom of a deep metal bowl, and Rupert was reading aloud from her book. He closed the book and stood up when Jake approached.

"June," Jake said. "Tie the horses to a stout tree. Make sure the leads aren't too low. We'll be in trouble if a horse was to get hurt."

"I know, Dad." She put the bowl on the table. "Thank you for breakfast, Dr. Grimm."

"There's more if you'd like when you get done with the horses."

"No, sir. I've had plenty. I'd like to talk more about 'Cupid and Psyche,' though, before we leave."

She got up from the table and took both lead ropes from her father. She looked around and found a suitable tree with thick limbs. She tied the horses high and close to the tree trunk to keep the leads from drooping down and tangling in their feet. She retrieved a stiff brush from her father's saddlebags and began to brush her horse's neck and back.

Jake sat at the table in her spot and looked at the fire.

"There's plenty more porridge here," Rupert said. "And I've got a coffee-pot sitting down in the coals."

"Thanks. I 'spect I better eat something. I hope you don't mind if we stay here until dark. The law'll be out looking for us and I don't want to travel in daylight. We can move on down the canyon and set up a little camp for ourselves if you'd rather."

"No. Please stay as long as you need to. I'd like to know where you're headed, though."

"I think I'd rather not say. No offense. You've been awful kind. June got most of a proper sleep this morning. It'll make today go easier for her."

Rupert chuckled. "I suspect that young lady'll have fewer difficulties today than either of us are likely to experience. She is…"

"Yeah, she's a toughie. Makes me proud."

"And she has a remarkable mind. The books she's read. Far ahead of other young girls her age."

"That's her mother's doin'. Sarah…she…" His voice caught, and he felt his eyes began to feel hot and scratchy. "She was always readin' to June and askin' her questions. Once June got to a certain age, I couldn't tell much what they were talkin' about."

"And still, you were married to June's mother for many years."

"I never did read much. Didn't finish school. Got where there didn't seem much point to it. There's things I can do, though. I'm good with my hands. Real good. But that didn't seem to matter much to folks at school."

"And your wife?"

"She didn't finish school either. But she knew all the school stuff better than people who'd been to all kinds of school."

Jake stopped talking. Somewhere in the forest nearby, he heard water trickling over rocks and looked away. A log in the fire burned in two and settled into the coals and a fragrant wisp of smoke brought Jake's attention back to the camp.

"But she?" Rupert said.

"Sarah knew books wasn't enough. I reckon that's why we kept June so close."

Rupert's hands began to tremble on the tabletop, so he clasped them tightly and put them in his lap. Jake had turned sideways on the bench to watch June brush the horses.

"I used to think books were enough," Rupert said. "I envy you, Jake. I still know barely enough to stay alive out here."

"They want to take her away," Jake said. "That's why we left home. Folks from the state, guy came all the way from Olympia and a woman up from Clarkston. They said June was gettin' behind. Said we had to put her in school. Said our place wasn't fit for raisin' a young girl."

"I should tell you…" Rupert started to speak.

"Tell me what?"

"I think I know where you're headed," he said. "And I don't think the law is going to be much a problem for a while."

"How could you know anything about us?"

"After you and June rode up over the ridge last night, I watched Tom Bennett take your truck and trailer down the road. I don't know where he was going, but I think he intended to mislead anyone who might come after you. Tom's a good man."

June had finished with the horses. She returned to the table and stood at the end with her father on one side and Rupert on the other. She picked up her book and held it close.

"You know Tom?" Jake said. "What else do you know?"

"I'd rather not say. No offense." Rupert grinned at June.

Jake was silent for a long moment, then he grinned. "I reckon I had that comin'."

"Yes, you did. I think you're traveling through the mountains to get to Ed Luke's cabin down in Oregon. You and Ed haven't got it finished, but it's habitable. And no one but you and Ed know where it is or even that anyone's been building a cabin."

Jake was stunned but said nothing.

"You know the way, but I know a shorter way. The cabin is closer than you think. It's just a little south of here in the next valley over. I can take you over the ridge and get you there in a couple of hours, but we've got to travel in daylight. The trail will be treacherous at night."

"How…do…How do you know all this?"

"I've got an old truck locked up at the trailhead at the downstream end of this canyon. I go to Pomeroy periodically to get supplies, check a book out of the library, that sort of thing.

"When I'm in town, I usually check in with Tom, give him an update on anything that might be going on down here. And there are people in Pomeroy I like to visit."

Jake turned back to face him. June slid onto the bench and sat very close to her father.

"Who do you visit, sir?"

"I've gotten to know Elsie Luke quite well. We met at the library."

"And Elsie knew…" June reached out and touched his folded hands.

He turned toward her. "And Elsie knew your mother." Then he turned his head toward Jake.

"That's how I met up with Sarah. Again."

*

Rupert's camp was at the far southern extremity of Garfield County, literally just yards from the Oregon border. At the opposite end of the county, some fifty miles from Rupert's camp, Ed and Elsie sat in a sunny nook that had been added on to the kitchen of their sturdy farmhouse. They ate breakfast, just as they'd done nearly every morning of their married life. As a rule, both rose before daylight and Ed would make coffee while Elsie cooked eggs and ham or bacon or mixed batter for flapjacks.

By the time they sat down to eat, the sun would be shining full force through the east-facing windows. Ed had hired Jake to add the breakfast nook to the house and install the windows. Elsie wanted the windowsill level with the tabletop so that the nook would be warm and bright in the morning regardless of the time of year.

Since Ed and Elsie were childless, their breakfast conversation usually covered farm matters. Projects to be completed. The progress of planting or harvesting. Issues with employees. What acreage should be sowed and which should be left fallow. The health of the livestock. The mechanical state of their machinery. Both had been brought up on successful farm and ranch operations and were of a similar mind on nearly every issue that mattered to the smooth operation of the ranch, so they never quarreled.

On the same morning June and Jake shared breakfast with Rupert Grimm, the breakfast dishes in the Luke place sat untouched on the small table in the sunny nook.

"Ed, I love that girl like she was my own flesh and blood," Elsie said. "But I don't think it's going to do her any good for Jake to take her away."

"The man's got a right to protect his family. That Crump woman sat right in our front room drinking our coffee, eating those cakes you made and threatened to take June and put her in a foster home until the court could decide if Jake and Sarah were fit parents. And she wanted you to help her do it."

Ed took a big swig of his coffee and frowned when he realized it was no longer hot. He took a deep breath and set the cup down.

"What you say might be true if Sarah were still…if Sarah was with Jake and June, but she's not. Without her mother, I don't know how Jake's going to manage with that child."

"No one in this county knows how that family has managed to live as well as they do. But they've managed. I reckon Jake will do just fine if folks like me and you and those goddamn bureaucrats will just leave them be."

She stood up with her untouched plate in one hand and began to take his plate with the other. She looked down at her husband. She drew her thin mouth into a tight frown then pursed her lips.

"I suppose you're right. But Crump might get a court order. CPS does it all the time. If Jake defies the law this time, things will just get harder and harder for June."

Ed reached out and took her free hand and squeezed it gently.

"I have never in thirty years left the breakfast table until I've eaten everything you've put in front of me. Don't see any reason that should change." He let go of her hand and took a drink of his now cold coffee.

"We got to figure out how we're going to manage the harvest without Jake."

Elsie returned to her chair and put a fork full of cold scrambled eggs in her mouth. She chewed slowly while Ed waited for her to respond.

"We'll figure it out. We always do."

Chapter 22

I began to wonder about Rupert the first time I saw him. I'd heard of hermits living in the mountains, but he didn't act like a hermit. His camp was orderly, and his clothes were of good quality. The kind my father wore. We always bought winter clothing after the harvest was done and Ed Luke paid my father. We never skimped on work clothes. They had to hold up.

But when I learned that Rupert knew or at least had met my mother, wondering turned to curiosity and curiosity to confusion.

While my father was grazing the horses, Rupert read to me from my book of myths. He asked which story I had most recently read, and I told the page number where the story of "Cupid and Psyche" began. But he did not immediately open the book to "Cupid and Psyche." He turned the first two blank pages over until he came to the title page and stared at the signature. He touched the page with his fingertips and frowned. Of course I'd seen the signature; I even asked my mother about it. But she said it was probably the name of someone who had owned the book before.

"What is it?" I asked him. "Page 149. That's where the story begins."

"Yes. Of course. Let's take a look. How many of these stories have you read?"

I was a bit perturbed by the idea that he thought I might not have read the whole book. "Why, all of them of course. I always read a book right through from start to finish. Then I like to go back and read the parts I really like again and again and…"

"Again," he said. "Yes. I like to read that way too. Do you ever read aloud?"

"Sometimes. When I don't understand right away."

"Good. You're not too proud or stubborn to say you don't understand."

He turned to page 149. His voice up to now had been unremarkable. But when he began to read, I recognized a familiar tone and an eerie change of pitch when a word or phrase needed to be emphasized. The recognition caused me to gasp loud enough for him to pause briefly and look up.

I heard a horse nicker and looked away in the direction my father had gone. He was on his way back to the campsite. I stood up quickly, put both hands on the table, and leaned toward Rupert.

"Why is Psyche not allowed to see her lover?" I had never heard myself speak with such urgency before. I felt my chest tighten and my chin begin to tremble. "Why does the god make her promise?"

"So, do you think it's the god who's responsible for Psyche's fate? And what about your mother?"

"My mother?"

He half stood and leaned forward to look me directly in the eye. He reached out and placed his right hand on my left. The panic began to immediately subside, and I sat down again. He removed his hand and nodded toward my father leading the horses up the trail.

"I'm sure your father will want to be leaving soon."

Later, while my father saddled the horses, I helped Rupert put out the fire with water from a stream that trickled out of the rocks a few feet behind the tent. We'd walk the horses up a narrow trail to the top of the ridge to the east of his camp. It would be steep, he said, but we could make it OK on foot in the daylight. The other side was easier, he said, and we may be able to ride down.

He stuffed two books and a thick loaf of bread into a leather shoulder bag and hefted it onto his left shoulder. He led the way to a wide spot in the creek down steam from the camp.

"Jake, you and June ride across," he said. "The water here's only about six inches deep, but there's no use getting your boots wet."

Rupert splashed across the stream and waited for us on the other side. My father looked at me and nodded. I climbed onto the back of my mare and rode carefully across the shallow stream. My father waited until I was safely across and then led his own horse across the stream on foot.

The trail was narrow and steep, but I don't remember the climb. Rupert had said… no… he had implied, that the god wasn't responsible for what happened to the princess. So… then… was God not responsible for what happened to my mother?

We neared the top of the ridge, and I could see Rupert standing at the crest. The sun had drifted to the south and cast a shadow across his face. He waved to indicate I should continue. But I stopped and waited for my father to catch up. His big gelding didn't manage the steep trail and the switchbacks as well as my smaller mare. My horse was anxious to complete the climb, so I put one hand against her chest and stroked her face with the other.

My father stopped when he caught up and leaned against my mare's hip. "We're almost to the top, June, keep moving. We'll rest at the top."

"I'm not tired." I recognized my voice, but the words came from some foreign place inside. My horse shifted her feet, and I had to dance sideways to keep my balance.

"What is it?"

I looked back to where Rupert stood fifty yards away, then I turned back to my father.

"Why did my mother die?"

Chapter 23

Rupert took two steps back down the trail. He stopped there and watched June and Jake from above.

Jake dropped his reins and moved carefully sideways on the narrow trail toward June. When he reached the girl, he was still standing downhill, so his face was level with his daughter's. He reached out as if to touch her cheek but placed his left hand on her right shoulder instead and set his jaw when he felt his lips begin to tremble. She reached up with her left hand and placed it gently on top of her father's right. She left her hand there for a moment and then took it away and stroked her horse's nose. Jake did not remove his hand from her shoulder.

"Your mom would've said there's some things in this life we just ain't supposed to know. Maybe she knows now."

June nodded. He took his hand away and backed down the trail, leaning on June's horse for balance, and picked up his reins. His own horse hadn't moved. June turned and led her mare to the crest of the ridge. Rupert stepped aside to let June and her horse pass. He placed his hand on Jake's shoulder and left it there until they reached a flat spot at the top where the horses could rest.

The top of the ridge flattened out to form a grassy clearing about a hundred feet along the crest of the ridge and fifty feet wide. June stopped when she reached the top. The men followed, and when Jake's horse reached June, Rupert took the reins of both horses and walked them to the far side of the clearing. He let the reins go slack so the horses could nibble the meager grass. Jake put his arm around June's shoulders, surprised again that the girl had grown to be at least as tall as her mother. She leaned in close to her father, and he guided her to a spot beneath a large tree.

He leaned against the tree and lowered himself until he was sitting on the ground. Jake leaned his head back against the tree trunk and closed his eyes. June slowly dropped to her knees and faced him.

"You can sleep a bit," he whispered. "If you need to, and it's OK to cry. I 'spect your mom wouldn't mind."

"I'm not tired, Dad. And I'm not going to cry. But you go ahead."

Jake opened his eyes and nodded. They watched each other, and June stroked the leathery skin on Jake's face with her fingertips. He tried but could not make his mouth form a smile. She stood up and walked away into the trees.

"I'll be back in a minute," she said. He started to warn her not to go too far, but she spoke before he could get the words out. "I won't go far."

He leaned his head back against the tree trunk again. She stopped a few feet away and looked back. Tears streaked the trail dirt on Jake's face, the only time she had ever seen her father cry.

On the other side of the clearing, Rupert stood between the horses and watched until June moved away, back toward the trail. Then he turned away. The ridge dropped off steeply where he stood. Across the empty space, he could see where the mountains resumed a mile or more away to the west. He took in a long deep breath and held it. His shoulders began to tremble, and he felt dizzy. He leaned forward with his hands on his knees to stretch his back and clear his head. He stood up and watched the clouds rise from the invisible valley floor far below. He folded his hands and placed them against his lips. He closed his eyes and contemplated the void stretching endlessly across the misty valley. When he opened his eyes, the clouds from the valley floor had risen high enough to obscure the mountains on the other side.

"Forgive me, Sarah," he said. He stood up and walked the horses back to where Jake was still sitting on the ground.

Jake looked up at Rupert and said, "Maybe we should've stayed home. Maybe we should go on back and see what they have to say. Maybe…"

June stepped out from behind the tree and took her horse's reins from Rupert. "Of course we shouldn't go home. *Doctor* Roberts and that Crump woman think I tried to shoot them."

Jake stood up.

"She's right," Rupert said. "You'll be at Ed's cabin in an hour, maybe less. The trail's easier on this side."

"Yes," she said. "We should get down the hill so we can eat and rest and feed the horses properly."

Jake smiled and shook his head.

"I'll be…" he said. His twelve-year-old daughter stood before him, but it was the clear and certain voice of Sarah that he heard. "Just like your mother."

*

With Rupert leading the way, Jake and June led their horses down the trail. The trail down was not as narrow or as steep, and there were fewer switchbacks. The trees were widely spaced near the top of the ridge, and there was almost no underbrush. The forest became more dense as they descended, and to June's surprise, the bottom of the trail didn't open into the familiar mountain meadow. Instead, the trail followed a narrow canyon, perhaps fifty yards wide, between two steeper hillsides. There was grass and vegetation she did not recognize in the ground cover among the trees, and the air seemed heavier. Instead of the clean sound of moving water and the soothing aroma of the pines, the hills were silent, and the air was eerily dank and humid. When Jill looked up, she could see intermittent blue among the gray clouds, but not the sun. She thought about getting on her horse for the last mile of their journey, but when she saw that Jake remained afoot, she decided to walk the rest of the way.

"Almost there," Rupert said after about twenty minutes. "Just stay on the trail between these two hills. You'll come to a meadow about a mile farther on. Ed's cabin is on the other side."

He turned back to face them. They were side by side now. "I suspect I should be getting back. I hope to see you both again sometime."

"You're not staying?" June said. "But the book, the story. You said we'd talk more about the story."

Rupert stepped forward and put a hand on each of her shoulders. She looked up and was stunned by the familiar smile that briefly brightened his face.

"Child, we'll talk again."

She nodded and led her horse around Rupert and down the trail. Jake nodded once at Rupert and then followed his daughter. Rupert started up the trail that would lead back to his tent. After a quarter of a mile, he changed his mind and headed for Ed's cabin by another route.

The trail ended at Ed's half-finished cabin. Jake and Ed had carefully selected the building site on the edge of a tiny bowl-shaped meadow between two very old pine trees. A noisy spring flowed over a rocky hillside and into a small pond in the center of the meadow. The cabin itself was constructed of heavy, rough-cut lumber with a broad porch and a steep roof. It looked finished from the outside, except there was no glass in the windows and no door. Single sheets of plywood covered the openings to keep the weather out, and June thought, *this will be at least as cozy as Rupert's tent.*

They led the horses around the edge of the meadow and tied them to a strong hitching post to the right of the cabin.

June wanted to see the inside, but first she removed a rope halter and a strong lead rope with a brass clip from her saddlebags. She removed her horse's bridle and tied the halter on. She tied her horse to the hitching post with a skillful slipknot and loosened the cinches, while Jake did the same for his horse.

She waited for her father to remove her saddle and set it on the hitching post. Then he unsaddled his horse and placed his own saddle next to hers.

"Let 'em stand here and relax for a bit," he said. "Then you can water 'em in the creek and I'll stake 'em out so they can graze. They done a nice job the last couple a days. Get your bedroll and we'll take a look inside."

She untied her blankets from the back of her saddle and followed him around to the front of the cabin. She was shocked to see a dirt track, deeply rutted by the wide tires of a truck, cut neatly through the trees. He stepped up onto the porch and turned back toward her.

"It's about half a mile down that track to the gravel road," he said. "But it's hard to see, and there's no reason for anyone to think we're here."

She continued toward the porch. She put one foot on the bottom step and looked up at her father.

"Where did Rupert go?"

Jake looked around casually. "I don't know. Back to his tent I 'spect."

"I thought he'd stay. I thought we might talk."

"He's done enough. We'll be OK from here on."

Jake put his own bedroll down on the porch and turned to the door. He grasped the thin plywood covering the door with both hands and pulled one side away easily. Then he pulled the other side free. He set the plywood flat on the floor of the porch, retrieved his bedroll, and walked in. The cabin had two rooms. The first doubled as a kitchen and living room, with a wood stove and a crude table with benches on each side. There was also a wooden couch against one wall. The second room, at the back of the cabin, contained four cots, each with a thin mattress rolled up at the foot.

"Bring your stuff back here," he said to June. "Pick a bed. It ain't like home, but it'll be better than sleepin' on the ground."

She put her blankets on the floor next to the cot closest to the boarded-up window. She unrolled the mattress and turned it over so it would lay flat. Then she spread her bedroll out and sat down.

"Um…there's no bathroom," he said. "But there's an outhouse in the back. The hole's plenty deep and it ain't been used this year. And there's firewood cut in the back, and those boxes by the stove is filled with enough food for a couple of weeks. Me and Ed was planning on doing the inside finish work after the harvest, if the weather didn't turn bad."

She nodded and said nothing.

"June, honey. Nobody but Ed and Elsie know where this place is and they're the only ones who know where we are. We'll wait here for a day or two. Just 'til Ed gets an idea of what Roberts and Crump might do about all this."

She continued to sit silently on the cot. He shifted his feet.

"When Ed thinks it's OK, he'll bring his truck and trailer down and we'll head north where I got people around Omak and Oroville."

She nodded.

"I don't 'spect they'll spend much time looking for us once we're outta sight. You never hit no one with that gunshot."

She stood up and walked across the room to her father. She stood directly in front of him for a moment then reached up and put her arms around his neck. He stood stiffly with his arms at his sides and waited.

She stepped away. "Jake, we're going to do what we need to do."

"You called me 'Jake.'"

"Yes. I did. Do you think Rupert will head back to his tent, or is he going to come back here to stay with us?"

Chapter 24

I didn't mean to hurt my father by calling him Jake. I hope he understands and forgives me.

So much of what this story is about has to do with forgiveness. What my mother was willing to forgive and what Crump and Roberts were not. My father didn't think about forgiveness one way or the other. He'd say holding a grudge is a waste of time and energy, not practical. And Rupert…he understood forgiveness more than anyone I ever knew, except my mother.

Do you know he doesn't travel down south in the winter anymore? He found a church in a small town in Oregon, and he teaches there every Sunday for half the year. They let him sleep in a room in the basement and pay him a little. But every spring he's back at his camp in the mountains.

"I study, so I'll have something to teach," he says. Rupert comes to visit me two or three times a year, but he never brings a present like Elsie. I do like to see him, though.

I made up my mind that I would forgive the people who put me here. The people who destroyed our family and separated me from my father and a way of living I was born and bred to.

Unlike my own sin, Crump and Roberts' transgression was not a lack of compassion, and they did not intend any deliberate harm. Their sin was simply a malevolent failure to understand.

So, I forgave them.

Crump and Roberts served an institution. And institutions have no soul, so it is inevitable their actions would be soulless. I hope they have forgiven me, even though my intention on that day was to harm one or both of them if I had to. I told the court the truth, that I would've done anything to keep them from taking my father.

I failed.

And that is why I'm here.

We spent the night in the cabin without Rupert. I don't know where he went or what he was doing. My father built a fire in the wood stove and heated up chili and green beans from cans he took from the boxes against the wall. We were so hungry, he had to heat up more of both. Then we each had our own can of peaches. I slurped the last bit from the bottom of the can, and the syrup dripped down my chin. I giggled when I saw the same thing had happened to my father. We both laughed, and he reached across the table and tousled my hair. That was the last time in my life that I felt like a little girl.

He had brought the saddles in from outside because he was afraid it would rain. He staked out the horses in the meadow. He wasn't sure they would stay close to the house otherwise, and if they wandered off, it would take time we might not have to find them. I took my book from my saddlebag, but the cabin was getting dark. My father had removed the plywood covering from one window in the front room, but he left the back room dark. When he saw I was trying to read, he found a flashlight and fresh batteries stored among the food boxes next to the wood stove and gave it to me. I took it and my book and lay down on my cot.

About an hour later, I heard him milling around. I got up and shone the flashlight into the front room, but he was not there. I turned it off and tiptoed to the open door. He was sitting on the steps with his Winchester lying across his lap.

"Dad?"

"It's OK, honey. I'm just waiting to see if Rupert comes back."

"Why do you have your rifle?"

"Just checkin'. Makin' sure it ain't got wet or dirty."

He moved the rifle from his lap and stood it up on the top step, butt down with his left hand on the barrel.

"June, I put your mom's .32 in your saddlebag. Make sure you can find it quick."

There was nothing more to say, so I carried my saddlebags to my cot and felt around until I found the small pistol. He always referred to the tiny handgun as belonging to my mother, but I had never seen her shoot it. I cocked it and eased back the slide to make sure there was no round in the chamber. I think Ms. Crump would've been horrified that I knew how to do this, but my father was as careful with firearms as he was with everything else. I lowered the hammer and reset the safety. I carefully placed the gun on the windowsill where I could get to it, although I could only imagine why I might need it. Then I remembered my father on the hillside, training his rifle sites on Tom Bennett, and I knew I would use the gun if necessary.

I lay on my back holding the book to my chest. I stared at the ceiling in the dark and thought for a long time about what Rupert had said about the princess and the god.

"She should've waited, June. Her miscalculation wasn't curiosity, it was disobedience and impatience."

My mother understood patience.

"We're all designed for glory," she once told Elsie.

"Designed?"

"Yes, Elsie. Designed. Engineered for a specific task."

"You make it sound so mechanical, Sarah."

"Not mechanical, divine."

Lying there on that cot in the mountains, it came to me. The human and the divine cannot connect until everything is just so. The princess was made for glory, but she was young, new in the world. The god *was* glorious. I began to nod my head slowly. *Made for glory*, I thought.

I realized then that the fate of the princess was a warning. I said the word over and over in my mind. *Patience. Patience. Patience.* And I turn eighteen tomorrow, so they have to let me out of here.

Chapter 25

om Bennett drove slowly on Highway 12 out of Pomeroy to the east. After two and a half miles, he turned on to a narrow two-lane road that would end after fifteen miles. It was situated on a well-tended, mile-and-half-long gravel lane that led to Ed and Elsie's modest farmhouse. The sign at the turnoff said *Luke Road,* a tribute not to the prominence of Ed's family, but to its longevity. He drove slowly because he didn't look forward to the question he had to ask Ed and Elsie.

"This is for the best, Sheriff," Roberts said. He was sitting in the front passenger seat of the Sheriff Department's SUV. Tom liked the larger vehicle much better than the department's late-model patrol car. It seemed to go with the county better, and out of towners were less likely to give him an argument when he pulled them over in the hulking four-wheel-drive vehicle. "You'll see. Ms. Crump has a great deal of experiences with cases like this. We only want what's best for the child."

"Is there any word on where the mother might've gone," Crump said from the backseat. "It's very curious that she should disappear after being so insistent about the child's lack of education."

Tom glanced in the rearview mirror to see Crump shaking her head.

"It's obvious from the looks of that house, this child is not being properly cared for," Crump said. "Why, she even had access to a gun. We're lucky not to have been shot, or worse."

"Ms. Crump," Roberts said. "I'm told these hill people usually have some experience with firearms. I'm not saying she should have access to a gun at her age, but…"

"Believe me," Tom said. "June knows how to handle that gun. If she'd wanted you shot, you'd a been shot."

In the rearview, Tom saw Crump open her mouth to speak, then close it quickly.

"Really, Sheriff," Roberts said. "You're not helping."

"Like I said before, don't mean to help, but I will do my job."

They traveled the rest of the way to Ed and Elsie's long gravel driveway in silence. When they turned off the paved road, with the house still not in sight, Crump said, "How far out do these people live? Are there no neighbors?"

"Except for the folks who live in town," Tom said. "'Most everyone in the county lives by themselves for the most part."

Ed and Elsie's driveway ran due north over several rolling hills and past alternating fields of dark summer fallow and ripening wheat for nearly a mile. The driveway was well maintained, so it lacked potholes, but Tom had to drive slowly to keep the truck's big tires from slipping on the gravel. Roberts watched the countryside roll by, impressed by the scale of the Lukes' operation. Crump stared straight ahead.

"What if something happens, an emergency? What if they need help?" she said.

"Well, there's the volunteer fire department, and me or my deputy can get most places in the county in less than thirty minutes. But mostly folks take care of things themselves. They've learned to do for themselves."

"I couldn't live like that," Crump said.

"No. I don't 'spect you could. Most of the help people get is after somethin' happens. Rebuilding if a barn burns. Or help with the harvest if someone's gotten sick or hurt."

"Has that girl's family ever needed help of that sort?" Crump said.

"Not that I'm aware of."

"I don't believe you, Sheriff."

Finally, the truck crested the last low hill, and the driveway bent gradually to the west and the house came into view. A neat, waist-high chain link fence surrounded Ed and Elsie's home, with a very large and very old oak tree dominating one corner of the sizable lawn. The house was square and plain, two stories and recently painted. A covered porch ran the entire width across the front of the house and the entire length of one side. Behind the house and slightly uphill was a large pole building with three enormous combines and three grain trucks parked outside.

The driveway appeared to continue past the building in back before disappearing into the wheat. Tom parked his truck in front of the house, and he and Roberts got out. They headed for the front door, but Crump did not move.

"Wait here," Tom said to Roberts just as they reached the gate. He walked back to his truck and tapped on the back window where Crump was sitting.

"You comin'?" he said. Crump rolled the window partway down. "You're the one with the court order."

"You're to serve the order," Crump said.

"Yep. That's right, but the document you gave me ain't for these folks. We're just goin' to find out if they know where Jake and June have gone to. You best come along."

"Sheriff, I'll not be told what to do."

"Yep. You will. You're in my county, and you asked for my help. I don't like any part of what you have in mind, so I guess you'll at least be there when I talk to these people. Why'd you ride all this way if you didn't intend to talk to Ed and Elsie yourself? Now, get out of the truck and come in with me and Roberts."

Crump did not move until Tom opened the back door of the truck and motioned for her to get out. She stepped down and sniffed the air. "What's that smell?"

"Oxygen. Come on now."

Tom led the way onto the porch. He knocked on the door and Elsie answered almost immediately. She greeted Tom with a friendly smile but then saw Roberts and Crump standing behind him.

"Well, this is a bit of a surprise," she said, no longer smiling. "Tom, what's this about?"

"Is Ed in the house? We need to talk to the both of you, if you've got the time."

"We're trying to get ready for harvest. Ed's in the shop. Without Jake's help, it's taking longer than it should to get the machinery ready." Elsie frowned at Crump and Roberts.

"I know, Elsie, but I'm afraid I'm going to have to insist a little. Can you get Ed down here for just a few minutes?"

"No need to insist. We can all walk up to the shop and talk in Ed's office."

Just as Elsie finished, she heard Ed come back into the house through the back door.

"Sounds like Ed's back in the house," Tom said.

She stood back and opened the door wider. "Come in. We'll talk in the kitchen. We've had breakfast, but there's coffee left." She stood aside, and Tom led Roberts and Crump down a short hallway to the kitchen. Crump was surprised the kitchen seemed to be by far the largest room in the house. Elsie followed.

"Please sit down," she said, and motioned Roberts and Crump to the table. "Would you like coffee?

Crump shook her head curtly and Roberts did not respond at all.

"Love some, Elsie," Tom said.

"Glad to see you've still got your good sense, Tom." She filled a heavy porcelain mug nearly to the brim and handed it to him.

He blew across the surface of the steamy brew and took a cautious sip. "Seems like the farther I get from town, the better the coffee tastes. You two really should have a cup."

"We won't be here that long," Crump said. "Mrs. Luke, we need to talk to you and your husband."

"Talk about what?"

Ed came in from the enclosed back porch that doubled as a utility room in the summer and mudroom during the winter and leaned on the doorjamb. Roberts stood up when he came in.

"Here's the thing," Tom said. "Ms. Crump is with CPS, as you know. Well, she managed to swear out a child endangerment warrant against Jake and Sarah and got some prissy-assed judge somewhere to sign off on it."

Crump started to speak, but Roberts put a hand on her shoulder, and she settled for a loud sigh.

"What does that mean exactly?" Elsie said.

Tom took in a long deep breath and let it out slowly. "What it means is I got to serve this warrant on Jake and these folks…"

"I'm just here as an observer," Roberts said. "I have no legal standing at this point."

"But you're here, ain't you," Tom said.

Ed gave Roberts a hard look. "Go on, Tom."

"I've got to serve this warrant on Jake, and these folks, I mean Ms. Crump here, will take June and put her in a foster home until the court determines if Jake…" He glanced at Elsie then looked away. "…if Jake and Sarah are fit parents and if their place is safe for a child to live."

No one spoke. Outside, the sound of a large diesel engine sputtered for several seconds and then rattled and started. Ed and Tom looked toward the sound. Elsie took the coffeepot from the stove and offered to refill Tom's cup. He shook his head. Crump cleared her throat.

"And what does this have to do with us?" Elsie said.

"We think you know where to find that girl," Crump said. She tapped the table twice with her closed fist.

Tom started, "If you know where Jake has taken June…"

"And if you know where the mother is," Crump said.

"You got to tell me," Tom said.

"I thought you went out to Jake's place?" Ed asked.

"Yes, sir. I did. His truck and trailer were gone along with the two saddle horses. I figured Jake'd head down toward the Oregon border. I drove down that way, looked around, and…Jake's rig ain't on any of the forest service roads. He may of turned off on one of the old dirt tracks."

"So, you don't know where June is?" Elsie asked.

Ed was silent.

"But we think you might know, Mrs. Luke," Crump said. "And if you do not tell the sheriff, there could be legal consequences."

Ed looked at Elsie and nodded toward the back porch.

"Excuse me," Elsie said. "I need to talk to my husband." She followed him onto the porch and closed the door.

Tom finished his coffee in one final gulp and poured himself another cup from the pot on the stove. Crump folded her hands on the table to wait, and Roberts pulled out a chair and sat down at the table next to her. After several minutes, Ed and Elsie came back into the kitchen.

"Meet us at Tom's office first thing in the morning," Ed said. "I don't know if they've gotten there yet, but I know where Jake's headed. Tom, you'd better call the sheriff down in Wallowa County."

"One thing first," Elsie said. "Until this gets settled, I want June to stay here with us."

"You'll have to agree to put her in school." Roberts stood up again.

"We don't have to agree to anything," Ed said.

"As far as we are concerned," Elsie said, "Jake can hide out in those mountains until hell freezes over, which it does most winters down there. But I don't think June needs this kind of trouble right now. If you'll let me and Ed take her in, we'll help you find them."

"Otherwise," Ed said. "You can deal with the Oregon authorities on your own."

"Of course, Elsie," Crump said. "We want as little disruption to the child's familiar routine as possible."

"It's *Mrs. Luke* to you."

Chapter 26

I don't remember ever sleeping past sunrise until this trip into the mountains. But when I woke up in the cabin, I could see flickering traces of daylight around the edges of the plywood nailed to the window. I could see my father's silhouette against the light pouring in through the front door. I got up, pulled on my jeans, and went to him in bare feet.

"Who's here, Dad? What is it?"

"You need to get your boots on. We're going back to Rupert's camp."

"Rupert? Is he here?"

"He was. Get ready now, it's late."

I pushed around my father and stepped onto the front porch. The sun was already above the ridge to the east, which meant it was very late in the morning…maybe nine or ten. Rupert was not there. I spun around, irritated and confused.

"How'd it get so late," I said. "Why didn't you wake me up? And if Rupert was here, where'd he go?"

"Seems like you needed the rest."

He put his hand on my shoulder, and I tried to shrug it off. He held on and steered me back into the cabin.

"Get your boots on. We need to get up the trail. Now."

I headed back to my cot but noticed both saddles were gone. The horses must've already been saddled and waiting for us at the hitching rail outside. I stepped into my riding boots and laced them as quickly as I could. I smoothed out my blankets, folded them over, rolled them up, and tied them into a tight bundle, so they'd fit neatly behind my saddle. I put my book and the flashlight in my saddlebag and started for the front door. I remembered the gun on the windowsill and went back for it. I started to stow it in my saddlebag but stuck it into my back pocket instead. When I got to the porch, my father was standing on the top step watching the dirt track that led out to the road.

"I'm going to tie my saddlebags and bedroll to my saddle."

"Good. Hurry." My father didn't move.

I went around the house and threw my bags and bedroll up behind the cantle. I had to stand on tiptoes to reach the tie straps. I tied the bedroll down on the near side and then went around behind my horse to tie the straps on the far side. Just as I finished and while I was checking to make sure the knots were secure, I heard a large vehicle drive up in front of the house. I stayed on the far side of my horse and did not move.

Three doors opened and then closed. After a long pause, the fourth door opened and closed. Then the sound of another vehicle, this one smaller and with the engine muffled drove up. This time one door opened and then closed. I came out from behind my horse and crept against the wall toward the front of the house. I peered around the corner and saw Sheriff Bennett and a man I did not recognize in a blue uniform. Behind Sheriff Bennett and the other policeman were Crump and Roberts and farther back next to Tom's Garfield County SUV were Ed and Elsie, who my father had said were the only people who knew where we were.

I leaned back against the wall and my hands were shaking, so I took two or three deep breaths to calm down. I reached behind my back and pulled out the .32. I pulled the hammer back to make the slide easier to operate and jacked a round into the chamber as quietly as I could. Ed must've heard because he looked my way but said nothing. I leaned back against the wall of the cabin and listened.

"Jake," Tom said. "I've got no choice here. These folks have got legal papers, and I got to serve them."

"I'm pretty sure you're in Oregon, Tom."

"We are in Oregon. That's why Sheriff Barnes is here. He can serve the papers, or he can arrest you and drive you back over the county line where I can serve the papers."

"That's the way you usually do things in Wallowa County, Sheriff Barnes?"

"If a child is in danger, yes sir."

No one said anything for a long moment.

"You think June's in danger, Tom? Elsie, how about you? Ed?"

Again no one spoke.

"No one thinks June's in danger except those two."

Crump spoke up, "In my experience…"

"You ain't got no experience when it comes to June."

Again silence.

"Jake," Tom said. "Why don't you go get the girl? Let things run their course. We'll do everything we can to make sure the state puts her in good hands."

"As long as she goes to school," Roberts said.

"Shut up, bureaucrat," Tom said. "You're just along for the ride, remember?"

"Well, Jake?" It was Elsie who spoke. "What are you going to do?"

"I'll go get her."

I did not move. I heard my father's footsteps as he walked back into the cabin. He returned immediately to the porch. As soon as he was through the door, I heard the unmistakable click-clack of the lever action on his rifle working.

"You folks need to leave," my father said. "June's not going with you."

Elsie spoke again. "Jake, they'll let June stay with me and Ed while this gets worked out."

"All I said, Mrs. Luke, is that we'd consider your offer to take the girl," Crump said. "I didn't agree to it. And the presence of that gun isn't helping this man's case."

I stepped around the corner and moved past the porch where everyone could see me. The gun was in my right hand and pointed toward the ground.

"I have a gun too," I said. I raised the .32 and pointed it at Crump.

"June! Don't!"

My father turned and took a step toward me. Tom and Sheriff Barnes jumped onto the porch and grabbed him. The rifle went off and the bullet buried itself in the cabin wall, and I turned my gun toward the scuffle on the porch.

"Get the girl," Roberts yelled.

He pushed Crump in my direction. She took two clumsy steps, then stumbled and fell, pushing me back against the porch railing. My finger tightened on the trigger of the .32. Crump's body muffled the sound of the gunshot, and she fell to the ground, bleeding at my feet.

*

Things happened pretty fast after I shot Crump. My father was pinned against the cabin wall by Sheriff Barnes. Tom leapt over the railing to see what could be done for Crump. Roberts retreated to a spot behind the horse trailer. Elsie came to me and put her arms around my shoulders. Ed took the gun from my hand. After a long time, an ambulance came, and Crump was taken away. The horses were loaded into Tom's trailer.

Sheriff Barnes handcuffed me and my father and put us in the backseat of his car. He, Tom, Ed, and Elsie talked for a long time. Tom and Ed took the horses back to Pomeroy or more likely to Ed and Elsie's place. I never knew what became of them. Sheriff Barnes drove us to LaGrande where my father was locked up in the county jail and I was locked into a small room with Elsie.

Neither of us spoke.

Sheriff Barnes said he understood why my father did what he did, so he didn't charge him with a crime. He explained to my father what was likely going to happen to me. And when my father left, he shook the sheriff's hand.

Because Crump didn't survive, I was sent to this special facility for female juvenile offenders, where I must stay until I turn eighteen, to be *rehabilitated*.

That's tomorrow.

I've never become familiar with the workings of the world away from our home. My movements have been strictly curtailed, but I've seen some of what that world can do, and I understand my mother's suspicion. I was not born on our place in the Blue Mountains, but I have only vague and infant memories of any other place. I do not remember spending even a day outside Garfield County, except to wander occasionally into Oregon on horseback while hunting cattle at the south end of our ranch. I've rarely spent a night away from the small room down the hall from where my mother and father slept.

My most vivid memory is of exalted silence and noble darkness. There was something substantial, elemental, even sacred, in the somber hush of night on our place. Not all light shone into the dark is revelatory. Sometimes knowledge obscures more than it reveals and gives the observer an inflated sense of importance. I am still certain there's more to the forest at night than is apparent even during the brightest day.

I never felt safer than standing on the new floorboards of the back porch in the moonless predawn hours the morning after we buried my mother. The dark was as complete as it had been on the early morning my father and I descended into the canyon where Rupert Grimm found us. It's early summer now and Rupert is certainly back out there in those mountains. Praying no doubt for us, my father and I. Praying for all of us. I'm still struck by the memory of our place. The silence of the mountains and the woods and of my mother's voice. I've never found the right scale to measure the weight of that silence, even though I've labored every day since to do so.

My life here has been well lit and attended by armed men. But I'm terrified every moment.

If I seem detached or apathetic when I speak of those days and of what I did, I apologize and beg forgiveness. It may be the chemicals. Or it may be that the flood of memory has drowned my reaction or that the inert nature of my life here has made me numb. Or it may be that the numbness is protecting me from a pain I will not allow myself to feel until I leave here and return to a better place.

My mother died.

She fell asleep on our back porch with a bowl of beans in her lap. I think she must have felt, as the last vague sensation of her time in this life, the slant warmth of the fading sun just before the eternal comfort of the welcoming dark enveloped her.

My mother died.

And I have spent all the years since trying to shine a light on that fact.

Also by Bruce Blizard - God's Instant

Available at …

Amazon (for Kindle and in Print):
http://www.amazon.com/Gods-Instant-ebook/dp/
B00CXSD2MA/ref=sr_1_1?ie=UTF8&qid=1382637270
&sr=8-1&keywords=god%27s+instant

On Bruce's website:
http://bruceblizard.com/

Can a desire for revenge lead to redemption?

Salvation doesn't always take place in church. God's Instant is the story of how two young people overcome the crippling effects of a missing parent and how a concrete connection with the recent past and exposure to a practical, bedrock faith in God brightens their future.

Set in the rugged deserts of southeastern Washington and the Blue Mountains of northeastern Oregon and against the exciting world of professional rodeo, God's Instant is the story of Jill and Grady. Jill has been hiding from the world in plain sight, and Grady is a brooding loner subject to periodic bouts of nearly homicidal rage. They're brought together by an enigmatic old couple possessing a determined and practical faith, and who, despite their own tragic past, refuse to live completely in the present.

What they're saying about *God's Instant*…

Jennifer Ciotta, Author and Editor at PenceyXPages:

A memorable and beautifully written story of a young cowboy and his search for himself and his past. Blizard's descriptions of the Washington countryside range from breathtaking to unusually haunting. As I read this book, I found myself immersed in the rodeo world and what it means to be a real cowboy. The story goes beyond the typical Western, tying in the struggles of adolescence and the theme of how to figure out where you're going, if you don't know where you come from.

Jim Deatherage, Award winning English teacher:

Barry Lopez, in CROW AND WEASEL, states, "Sometimes a person needs a story more than food to stay alive." Bruce Blizard's intriguing novel, GOD'S INSTANT, is just such a story of sustenance, drawing together everyday folks adrift in hidden secrets, brutal honesty, unrealized connections, and hope.

Prologue

O ld rodeo hands say you can tell whether or not a boy will grow up to be a bull rider by the look in his eyes after his first ride. If he can contain the dark fear that is the bull rider's necessary companion, if he can leave the terror buried in a safe place behind his eyes, the boy will most likely ride again. If he can't, and the fear rises to the surface as he sprints wide eyed and open mouthed toward the arena fence, his first bull will usually be his last.

The young cowboy had managed to bury the fear deep and hold it down for so long, he was no longer aware the fear was there. For that reason, he was in mortal danger every time he climbed into the chute.

*

Most of the southern half of eastern Washington State was eternally brown. Sage brush and prairie grass gave the rolling hills the same bland quality young people ascribe to the very old. At first cattle thrived on the land and then wheat and apples, and now grapes grew with abundance. From the crest of Rattlesnake Ridge or the Horse Heaven Hills, the reactors of the Hanford Nuclear Reservation were visible. Hanford, known as "The Site" to local people, was once a nuclear weapons factory. It remained one of the most technologically advanced and dangerously polluted places on earth.

A young man stared at the ancient landscape through a grimy window of a small house. In the distance behind Rattlesnake Ridge, he could see a sinister column of steam rising from the cooling towers at Hanford. He squinted against the pale light reflected off the Yakima River and onto the face of his sleeping son. When the child turned onto his back, away from the light, his father bent down and kissed him on the forehead.

The boy's father had risen early to pack his old pickup with the gear necessary for another rodeo journey. When he went outside to start his truck, the rattle of the diesel engine woke his young wife. She pulled on a pair of old jeans and shuffled into the kitchen to say goodbye to her husband.

"Do you want breakfast?"

"No, don't bother. A little hunger will keep me alert."

"How long this time?"

"Four or five weeks if I'm winnin' any cash. I'll send money when I can."

"You always do."

She kissed him on the lips.

"I worry, you know."

"I'm still young. I heal up fast."

"If you break something, you'll have to come home."

"You'd like that."

She smiled. "I love you."

"Take care of the boy."

"We need you."

"I'll be home when I'm done."

He put his arms around his wife. After a moment he nudged her away and walked out the back door. He climbed into the warm cab of his truck and rolled down the driver's side window and breathed in the cold air.

The young woman stood over the sleeping boy and watched the truck turn left onto the two-lane blacktop and disappear. She didn't know he would not return, not for a long time.

Chapter 1

Grady grasped the heavy steel bar that braced the two ends of the chute, bent his knees, and settled back into a deep stretch. He stared into the long chute at the broad, round back of a two-thousand-pound bucking bull, whose obscene hump rose and fell with each angry breath.

Suddenly, Grady felt very cold. He raised his eyes for a few seconds, gazing at the hard blue sky above the grandstand.

"Okay?"

"Yeah. I'm ready."

Grady stepped down into the chute. His world contracted, squeezed by a familiar, primal fear. For an instant his guts churned with the certain knowledge he might be seriously injured and with the tacit understanding he might even die. Beneath the bull's broad back and beyond, the confines of the chute was nothing but an eternal drop into the abyss. He pushed away the fear and straddled the bull. He sat down carefully, feeling the muscles of the animal's back bunch up. The bull was preparing to launch him out of the abyss toward the timeless blue sky. He got a good grip, took an extra wrap on the heavy bull rope, and pulled himself up as far as he could toward the bull's hump with his gloved right hand. He pressed his white hat farther down on his head, dropped his chin, and nodded.

The bull leaped sideways and began to buck and twist to the left. Grady thought he'd lost his hold on the first jump, but his grip remained when the bull changed direction and began to spin to the right. He squeezed hard by using the young muscles in his thighs. The fear in his guts abated again, and he stayed on.

Chapter 2

Grady Cross was eighteen years old and had never graduated high school. He perched on the curb in front of a truck stop near the freeway in the college cow town of Ellensburg, Washington. He was waiting for someone to offer him a ride south. He came within a second of winning a check at the Ellensburg Bull-O-Rama earlier in the day. But a hard rain, unseasonable for early September, fell steadily before he got on the last bull of the afternoon. He lost his grip when the big, gray monster twisted to the left instead of to the right as Grady had expected.

He was airborne when he heard the eight-second buzzer go off. He raised his head after splashing down in the soggy arena and saw the bull pawing the muddy ground about ten feet away. He rolled to the left and stumbled to his feet as a bullfighter raced in front of the heaving animal. Grady saw the bullfighter's painted face as he darted between Grady and the bull. The bullfighter planted his left hand in the center of the charging bull's forehead and vaulted past Grady like a desperate gymnast. The enraged animal's lethal head followed the bullfighter. The crowd cheered. He remembered thinking if he'd lasted just one more second, the cheers would have been for him and not for the bullfighter who had saved him from being gored, or much worse. Maybe he'd do better when he returned for the big-time Ellensburg Rodeo at the end of the month.

Grady was tall for a bull rider, nearly six feet, but he had the look otherwise. Big hands with sinewy fingers and strong shoulders that triangled up from his waist. His legs were longer than they needed to be, but he was sturdy, and the muscles of his thick thighs strained the fabric of his fading Wranglers. His leather belt was decorated with a dozen silver stars and was held together just below his naval by a tarnished buckle. It was no fashion statement, though. Without the belt, his Wranglers would slide off his narrow hips. Except for the tightness in his thighs, all of Grady's clothes seemed too big.

The rain had stopped, and the late afternoon sun was shining. The mud on his shirt and jeans had dried and mostly dusted off, but he was still sore, tired and lonely. He needed to get home for a few days. In a couple of weeks, he'd try to catch a ride to Pendleton for the big rodeo. He wore his long duster, a canvas raincoat that was split partway up in the back for riding a horse. It had kept the rain off, and he was happy to have the setting sun to warm the soreness out of his shoulders and arms and dry most of the dampness out of his boots.

At last, an old man offered him a ride in a sagging, rusted flatbed. It carried a load of hay in the back and had a big dent in the left front fender. The old man had filled the truck with gas and was checking his load, making sure the tarp that covered four tons of neatly stacked hay was secure. That was when he noticed Grady. He moved stiffly and without grace, but with purpose. This meeting with Grady was no accident.

"Need a ride south?"

"Yes sir, I do," Grady said, rising quickly to his feet. He straightened his duster and gathered up a small riggin' bag that contained his bull rope, thick leather chaps, and riding gloves.

"Well, hop in. I'll be right back."

Grady removed his long duster and hefted it and his riggin' bag into the backseat of the truck. Then he leaned against the front bumper, while the old man finished checking the tarp and paid for his gas.

"How far ya goin'?" the old man asked when he returned to the truck. He knew the answer.

"I'm headed home to Richland. I've been rodeoin'."

"You don't have a horse, and not much riggin' and you're pretty well covered with dirt, so I'll say you musta been tryin' to ride a bull."

"Ah, yes sir. I guess it shows." Grady noticed the old man had coarse white hair sticking out from under a rumpled cowboy hat. He also had a deep scar on his left cheek, and he looked vaguely familiar.

"I ride bulls, broncs sometimes, when I can manage entry fees for both and can borrow a bronc saddle. Almost won some money today. Sucker zigged, though, and I zagged about ten feet in the air."

Even though he already knew much of the young bull rider's story, the old man let Grady talk. He listened and said nothing. When Grady was done, the old man turned away and stared off to the south long enough to make Grady feel uneasy. Then, just as Grady was having second thoughts about accepting the man's offer of a ride, a smile creased his weathered face.

"So, you're the boy that got dumped so hard there at the end?" the old man asked. "I know an ol' boy workin' the pens. I was back there when you loaded up. That was a tough bull. I didn't think you'd get out of the chute. You did alright with that bull, son."

Grady was confused, but he appreciated the compliment. Still, the first thing he'd learned about the rodeo was that staying on for seven seconds and getting bucked off on the first jump looked the same to the woman at the pay window.

"Tough way to make a living but might as well do it while you're young enough to survive," the old man said. "It gets hard later on."

His eyes were set deep and dark, and his mouth had the stiff set of someone used to things being hard. His knuckles were scarred. Grady sensed he wasn't talking about riding bulls.

"I appreciate the ride," Grady said. "How far you goin'?"

"I can take you as far as Benton City. I got a place a little north and west of there. 'Bout a thousand acres. A few dozen cows. Some horses. No neighbors for a good long ways."

"That'll be fine. I can call my mom, and she'll come out from Richland and get me." *A few nights in my old room sleeping in my own bed would not be bad at all*, Grady thought.

"I don't mind the company."

A thin cloud of white smoke and the oily odor of diesel exhaust briefly filled the cab. It dissipated when the old man put the truck in gear. Grady climbed in, and the old man pulled onto the main roadway.

"My name's Grady." He extended his hand, but the old man did not take it.

"Yeah Grady, I reckon I know who you are." He held tight onto the steering wheel and stared straight ahead as they left the gas station. He pulled onto the interstate and headed south. Grady turned away and sat back in the hard seat. He fidgeted, unable to get comfortable. He was used to rodeo people knowing who he was or rather knowing who his father was and what he had done.

"I don't guess you got to take me along if you don't want to," Grady said.

The old man ignored him. "I'm John. Hope you're not in a rush. This old rig'll get us there, but we ain't goin' to hurry. You just relax, and I'll get you home by and by."

John's name and his face began to form an indistinct image in Grady's memory, but he was too tired to say any more. He settled back into the seat and stared at the withered landscape rising in front of him. Sagebrush, prairie grass, large rocks here and there. The highway climbed south away from Ellensburg up the first of three tough grades to the top of Manastash Ridge. Grady always made it a point to look back here to see the long, broad, green checkerboard that was the Kittitas Valley. The lights of Ellensburg would be visible in twilight. The valley drifted west and then curved suddenly northward toward the Cascade Mountains, which were already changing from deep green to black in the shadows of the approaching night. This time when Grady turned to look, the load of hay in the flatbed blocked his view. So, he missed seeing the landscape, but he did enjoy the faint odor of newly cut alfalfa.

"I wish I could sleep, but it's hard right after a rodeo," Grady said. "I'm plenty sore and tired. Ever rodeo yourself?"

"Nope. My boys did. Oldest's a pretty good roper too. Never made much of it, though. It's hard when you have to make a livin' to rodeo at the same time. The youngest did it all at one time or another. Rough stock at first, bareback, saddle bronc, bulls now and then. Scared his mother to death. She was happy he gave it up and took to calf roping. He won some money ropin' calves."

"What do your boys do now?"

"The oldest doctors cows in a feed lot or works for farmers and ranchers around home once in a while. The middle boy, he lives somewhere down around Boise with his wife some a' the time. Don't know what he does the rest a' the time. He don't bother to get up this way too much. Youngest is dead."

"Dead?" Grady wanted to ask how John's son died, but he was suddenly very sure he knew. The indistinct image in his memory coalesced into a name and a face that made his heart race. He didn't say anything.

"Yeah. I reckon he was about your age when it happened."

Grady sat up and turned toward him. "You're John Carpenter."

The old man continued to stare straight ahead. The dark was nearly complete, and the landscape rolled past in shades of green sage and brown sand that faded to black as night settled. The sky was the deep blue people in town never see, almost black but with a suggestion of color that would remain until long after the moon and the stars came out. In the desert, it would not be fully dark until just before the sun came up.

"I am," John answered.

He was silent for a long time.

"But it don't make no difference."

Grady turned away and focused his attention on the steep landscape darkening in the twilight. They passed through several miles of dark prairie before John spoke again.

"Look, son, I know who you are. Fact is I knew it when I picked you up. And you know who I am. Won't do neither of us no good to say it out loud. Just sit back and get some rest. What's done can't be changed. And that's the end of it."

"I won't blame you if you leave me off down the road here. I 'spect I can get another ride."

"No need. Don't say no more. I'm happy to help you out."

Chapter 3

Jill Marion was only fourteen when the accident that killed her father and nearly ended her own life left her mother an emotional invalid. When she walked home from school every day, now three years later, she had no sense of going home, only of going away. On this day, it was raining when she left school. But twenty minutes later, when she arrived at the house she shared with her mother, the rain had stopped.

Jill lived on a shady street in Richland, Washington. But today the trees that normally provided slight relief from the searing summer sun dripped and drooped in the wake of three days of unending rain.

She did not take her oversized hood down after she walked through the front door. The house was not tightly constructed. A faint musty odor that reminded her of an old woman's house replaced the normal, summertime dustiness.

Her mother was asleep on the couch, so Jill covered her with a heavy afghan and kissed her on the forehead. She sat in a big armchair that faced the front window and watched the trees drip and the afternoon shadows change as it turned dusk. She laid her head back against the chair and decided that there was no point in staying any longer. She would leave tonight.

*

In this particular strip of the extreme northwest corner of the US almost everyone, including Jill's mother and dead father, came to the desert from somewhere else.

The rain of recent days was a welcome change to the normal cycle of alternating hot and cold dry spells. The land had once been good for cattle and little else, then the college farmers at Washington State University taught the ranchers to irrigate the land, and the cows grudgingly gave way to apple and cherry orchards. The farmers and ranchers alternately prospered or struggled, thriving in the good years and either starving or selling out in lean times. Finally, opportunists from elsewhere gradually discovered that grapes provide more money and less uncertainty. So, vineyards surrounding ornate wineries had begun to creep up the sandy, treeless hillsides and crowded the tiny towns. The land was dry and dusty—barren except where the dams on the Columbia and the Snake rivers and the endless miles of narrow irrigation canals brought water.

Even where the land was irrigated, a lot of the ground here wasn't good for much of anything but cows. Long ago, and occasionally even now, scattered herds spotted the dry hillsides. They foraged for grass and held their own, waiting for a date with the feedlot and the slaughterhouse. Then one day, when the rest of the country was slugging its way through the dark middle years of World War II, the US Army came and found a darker purpose for a dusty crescent tucked into a slow bend in the Columbia. The government decided in 1943 that this land of few people, sparse crops, scant prosperity, and three rivers was the perfect place to build a huge nuclear bomb factory. The tiny burg of Richland—once situated precisely where the Yakima slides across a muddy delta into the Columbia—became a boom town. And the resulting nuclear roar had never been silenced.

Locals called the Hanford Nuclear Reservation "The Site." It sprang fully formed from the desert and from the mind of a determined and single-minded Army General named Leslie Groves. The chemical remnants of the necessary horrors created in secret there continue to haunt the region. The nuclear nightmares of Hiroshima and Nagasaki, the mad logic of deterrent strategies during the Cold War, and the legacy of poison, which exploded downward and seeped toward the Columbia River at the dawn of the present century, all had their genesis when a General Groves discovered the parched land was good for death too. The people who had long before settled in the desert were at first bewildered by the change wartime necessity brought to their home, but they generally embraced the prosperity that came with the Hanford Nuclear Reservation and mostly moved quietly out of the way. In their place, a scattered tribe of scientists, engineers, and technicians, that would eventually include Jill's father, assembled and put down shallow roots.

People in the inland northwest never developed the habit of dissimulation, even after the scientists arrived, because the people here didn't have time to invent tall tales. Wrenching a living out of the sand and rock was so difficult that embellishment had not seemed necessary. The culture of science brought to the desert by General Groves resisted exaggeration. The region had a dualistic mythology: the scientific hubris that came from a new age belief in the power of technology and the glory of the reactors, and an old-timey faith in the resilience of the land and in the cleansing power of the endless wind and the great rivers.

At the heart of this mythology was the Columbia River. Once swift and cold, but now deep and no longer wild, the river had been calmed, like much of the countryside. But there remained just beneath the surface an uncertainty bred in the union of an ancient land and a mysterious future.

*

Jill had lived here all her life, so she was not interested in either tall tales or nuclear realities. Generally, it was people who lived elsewhere who concerned themselves with life in the shadow of the Hanford reactors. At seventeen, Jill had enough to do. She lived with the loss of both parents, one dead and one in a daze.

"We'll have to help each other now," Her mother told her while Jill lay in a hospital bed on the day of her husband's funeral. "We only have each other now." The memory of those words at first made Jill sad then angry, and finally, resigned. After her father died and her mother had all but removed herself from Jill's world, the girl became silent.

Jill sat in a large chair until long after the sun had set, and the room had grown dark. Outside light rain pattered against the windows. She had not taken off the long wool coat she wore to school every day, regardless of the weather. She pushed back the oversized hood. It draped over the back of the chair to reveal a wet tangle of brown hair. At school, she wore the coat buttoned nearly to her chin, with the hood pulled safely down. It was difficult to see her eyes.

Once she had made up her mind to leave, she pulled the hood back over her head and down so her eyes became invisible again. Her mother remained asleep on the couch. She had not moved. Jill left the house and went out into the rain, into the dark.

She followed a route she knew well. She walked six blocks north, cut through a wooded area next to the middle school, sloshed across the school's broad expanse of green playfield, and headed east toward the river. The Columbia at Richland was flat, deep, and slow. During the hot and sunny summer months, the calm channel was busy with jet skis and power boats. On shore oily teenagers preened for each other, while wary young mothers guarded toddlers who splashed in the shallow water. But on this rainy autumn evening, the river and the long green line of General Leslie Groves Park were both deserted. The rain made the surface of the river seem alive with countless tiny ripples, perfect watery circles that expanded then disappeared as they moved away to the south with the slow current.

She was familiar with both the river and the park. She had spent many hours there in the three years since the accident, usually at night and always alone. She had been asleep in her father's car when it flipped on the freeway in the middle of the night. But when she woke up in a hospital bed after three days, her only memory was of her mother telling her that they were alone and would have to rely on each other. She did not attend her father's funeral. Her mother never talked about the details of the wreck, and Jill never asked, even though she often searched vainly for any memory of that night. The details of the wreck did not seem to matter, but hearing her mother talk about the accident did. With her father dead, and her mother silent, she was alone.

She sat on a damp bench at the river's edge. The light of a distant streetlamp cast a rippling shadow on the water. She lowered her head. Raindrops dripped off the scant leaves drooping from the tree limbs that hung low above her bench and mixed with the tears that had begun to fall again. They fell together onto the warm, blue fabric of her faded jeans and widened into wet circles. She stared at the river as it flowed by, nearly invisible in the dark. She squeezed the tears from her eyes as her body began to shake with grief and cold. She hugged herself to steady the rising panic and to warm the dampness from her bones.

She began to rock back and forth on the bench. She tried to calm herself by imagining her father and conjuring up memories of a man who played with her and bought her books and toys and carried her on his shoulders. But nothing was vivid, nothing she could see clearly and certainly. It was as if a dense fog had rolled across her recollections, and without a clear picture of her past, she could not imagine a future.

The rain had stopped again, but the tears continued to stream down Jill's face as the surface of the river settled and flattened out. The Columbia remained the color of slate, where the streetlights, which illuminated the asphalt pathway running north and south parallel to the river, did not shine on the dark water.

She stared at the current and felt a familiar and irresistible tug, a strong pull that seemed to extend from the depths of the channel to another place deep inside her. She resisted as she always did. But this time either the pull was too strong, or she was too tired, so she gave in.

She stood and walked carefully on the wet, downward slope to the very edge until the quiet water soaked the toes of her shoes. The tears had stopped, and she stepped into the river. The cold shocked her awake, but she continued. Still in the light of the streetlamp, she felt the slow current nudge her downstream as the water reached her waist. She was completely in the dark by the time the water reached her chin. She inhaled and let the river take her away. It covered her head, and she stroked for the bottom. She turned over once and was surprised that the streetlight was dimly visible from beneath the surface. Tightness in her chest and a deep, burning sensation caused a sudden and unexpected sense of panic. She discovered she was struggling for the surface. She tried to find the river bottom, but when she pushed her feet down, it was not there.

She stroked for the surface, but her heavy coat made it nearly impossible to move her arms. The pressure of the water forced the oversized hood down against the top of her head and over her face, blocking the diminishing glare. She pushed the hood back off her face and struggled toward the streetlight. An image of her father flashed across her mind. He was frowning and seemed to be disappointed in her. A few moments before, she had been standing on the riverbank where death seemed a welcome relief. Now terror and panic flooded her mind. Her lungs continued to burn, and the light continued to fade even though she strained to keep her eyes open. Finally, she felt herself drifting away. She reached once more for the surface, but she had no strength left. She ended the struggle that had begun the night her father died. The girl closed her eyes, and with a sob, exhaled and surrendered to the river.

Her body floated to the surface. The current banged her into a dock behind a new hotel on the riverbank. The force of the collision against her back turned her over and forced her to cough at the same time. Dark water burned her throat as it escaped her lungs. The girl reached out and grasped the dock with one arm. She reached up with the other arm and was able to get a hand around the thick rope that rimmed the edge. She rested there for several minutes before easing her way to the middle of the dock, where a three-step ladder extended down into the water. Jill found the bottom rung with her left foot, and with a great effort, shrugged off the coat. She watched it sink as the current took it away. She put her right foot onto the next rung and stepped up and out of the river onto the dock. She was on her hands and knees, and her body was shaking when everything she had eaten during the day came up in one long eruption. Her head sagged toward the remnants of her junk-food lunch. The pungent, chemical odor of digestive fluid mixed with a badly chewed hotdog and a blue goo that had once been a blueberry Slurpee burned the inside of her nose. She retched again. When she was done, she rolled onto her back, away from the putrid puddle and felt light.

She stretched out and stared at the moon peeking through the thinning clouds. She closed her eyes and took in two or three deep, cool breaths, ecstatic that she could feel the damp river air flowing easily into her lungs.

*

Everyone who lived in the desert near the Columbia in the days before the dams and the reactors had a river story to tell—of flood or fire or both. Stories of damnation or redemption. Occasionally of salvation. After her father died, Jill was irresistibly drawn to the river. She seemed to know that when the time came, the river would take away the pain of being alone.

When he was much younger than Jill, John Carpenter loved to travel to the river with his father from their home on the Roza, west of Benton City, and midway up the slope toward Rattlesnake Ridge. They would journey on horseback through their scattered herd and across the sage prairie as it leveled out between the grassy rise of the ridge and the noisy progress of the Yakima River. To the north and west was the barren hulk of Rattlesnake Mountain, the tallest mountain in North America without a tree on it, or so a persistent local legend insists. The ride took most of an entire day and brought father and son to the sharp southern bend in the Yakima, where the ridge leveled into a broad plain three miles wide that stretched to the Columbia farther east.

In those days the Columbia was narrow and swift. The river had not yet been dammed to satisfy the thirst for water and the demand for power of people far distant from the desert and far removed from its life. At this southern limit of the Hanford Reach, John and his father would dismount, unsaddle, and let the horses graze on the moist, green grass that grew at the river's edge. They would fish and eat, but the river moved too fast for swimming. Still, the long ride was hot, so John would remove his clothes and wade naked into the current up to his thighs. The cold, rushing water carried away the heat and fatigue from his feet and legs. He'd lie down in the warmer water that eddied near the shore to cool his sun-baked skin.

The Columbia River was alive in those days, and the bank on both sides of the river was verdant and lush. The prairie stretched flat near the water's edge then up and away in all directions, brown and dusty in the summer heat. After a warm night on the riverbank, John and his father would saddle up again in the morning and ride home, back over the ridge or across the prairie and along the Yakima if the weather was hot. Some years later John explained the river's old flood cycle to a newcomer. "Twice some years in the old days, the Columbia spread out over its banks a mile on each side."

With the Columbia in flood, the Yakima seemed to shrink. Today, the Columbia did not flood anymore, but the semi-wild lower reach of the Yakima River retained its redemptive force and native cleansing power.

*

Jill finally sat up. Her oversized clothes, khaki pants, and a thin, long-sleeve shirt clung to her narrow body. Her straight hair was stuck to the back of her shirt. She felt exposed without her long coat and without the protection of her hood, so she pulled her knees toward her chest and hugged her thighs. She began to shake and shiver with terror and cold. She stumbled to her feet and walked stiffly up the ramp and off the dock. It was late, and the rain had stopped for good. She encountered several other kids walking along the paved path.

"Hey, it's the Creature from the Black Lagoon," one boy said then laughed.

Jill said nothing.

"Kind of cold for a swim, ain't it?" The boy said as he brushed by her. Several others laughed and ran off through the trees and into the park. She heard the roar of an engine starting and tires squealing as a car sped out of the park and back into town.

Jill hugged herself as the shivering increased. She headed through the park the same way the others had gone and stayed off the well-traversed streets. Within two blocks of her house, a green-and-white police car pulled up to the curb beside her. She did not stop, but a policeman got out of the car and began to follow her.

"Excuse me. Can I talk to you for a second?"

She stopped and turned toward the policeman who was several steps behind her. He was tall like her father. His face was familiar, and he had a gentleness to his voice that nudged a blurred image from the night of the wreck across her memory.

"What did you say? I just thought…"

The policeman was next to her before she could continue. The chill was still with her, but she had stopped shaking. She kept her arms wrapped around herself as tightly as she could. She was determined not to let go.

"I'm on my way home, officer," she said.

"How'd you get so wet?"

Her mind seemed to have slowed down along with everything else. She did not answer right away. She trembled and said, "I fell in the river. I'm a little cold. I need to get home."

"Someone called us to say there was someone passed out on the float down there. Was that you? You look a little familiar. Do I know you?"

She did not answer.

"Do you need any help? How far away do you live? What do you need? A ride?"

Jill waited. "No. I live just down the street here. I'll go home and get warm."

"I better drive you. Get in."

"No, really, no."

She tried to run the last block to her house, but all she could manage was a stiff shuffle. The policeman got into his car and followed slowly. When Jill finally reached the walkway to her front door, the police car stopped at the curb again, and the officer followed her to the small porch.

"I'm okay now. Really. I just…"

"I better talk to your folks." He knocked on the door.

"Please. My mom's asleep."

"You look like you've had some trouble. I think I better have a talk with her. Is your father home?"

Again, Jill did not answer. She turned away from the door and leaned against the wall She began to shake again. The damp air and her wet clothes seemed to merge.

"Please, officer, I'm okay. I don't want my mom woken up. She… she works all the time and…and I'm okay really. Please."

Jill was surprised when the man reached out and gently stroked her cheek. She flinched a little. But when he took his hand away, she remembered the warmth of her father's fingertips on a rainy day, a spot of relief from the cold. Again, the same indistinct image of her father crossed the girl's mind, and for an instant, while the memory remained, the cold dissipated.

"Well, okay. If I were your dad, I'd want to know what happened. But you don't seem to be harmed much, just cold. Right?"

"Believe me, my dad won't care. And my mom needs her sleep."

"Alright, you go inside and get warm. Maybe I'll check on you in the morning."

"Thank you."

The policeman turned away, headed back down the narrow walkway, and got into his car. She had entered the house before he pulled away. On the couch, her mother was still asleep, as Jill had left her. She was nearly undressed by the time she reached the bathroom. She piled her wet clothes in a heap outside the door and stepped into a scalding shower. She shuddered once then cried quietly. The hot water brought life back into her limbs as it rinsed the cold tears from her face. She let the water run over her for a long time before she got out and dried off.

She crawled naked into her small bed and pulled the blankets over her head to hide her face. She slept hard and for a long time.

And she dreamed.

The rain was coming down so hard she was having trouble breathing. She seemed to be a long way from home, but she was soaked and walking down the last block to her house. Finally, the policeman who had followed her home rescued her. But he was not in his uniform. He was dressed like her father on the night he died.

The dream woke her. She sat up and blinked at the glare from the streetlight outside her window and went back to sleep.

And she dreamed again.

This time the rain had stopped, and it was very hot. She was wearing the thick, hooded coat she had lost in the river. Though there was no sun in the dream, the heat was causing steam to rise from the coat. This time her father himself approached her.

"Don't be afraid, sweetheart. It's not so bad after a while."

When Jill woke up the sun was shining, and she could hear her mother moving about in the kitchen. For the first time in as long as she could remember, she felt rested. She kicked off the blankets and stretched. She got up, put on a thin robe, and walked into the kitchen.

"Mom?"

"How'd your clothes get so wet?"

"Uhhh…"

"Never mind. I've got a surprise. I think we need a change."

"A change? Mom?"

www.ingramcontent.com/pod-product-compliance
Lightning Source LLC
Chambersburg PA
CBHW061300210726
48293CB00003B/1051